THE NIGHT WE GOT STUCK IN A STORY

BEN MILLER

THE NIGHT WE GOT STUCK IN A STORY

SIMON & SCHUSTER

First published in Great Britain in 2022 by Simon & Schuster UK Ltd

1 3 5 7 9 10 8 6 4 2

Simon & Schuster UK Ltd
1st Floor, 222 Gray's Inn Road
London
WC1X 8HB

www.simonandschuster.co.uk
www.simonandschuster.com.au
www.simonandschuster.co.in

Simon & Schuster Australia, Sydney
Simon & Schuster India, New Delhi

A CIP catalogue record for this book is available from the British Library.

HB ISBN 978-1-4711-9249-4
TPB ISBN 978-1-3985-1751-6
PB ISBN 978-1-4711-9250-0
EXPORT ISBN 978-1-3985-1986-2
eBook ISBN 978-978-1 4711-9251-7
Audio ISBN 978-1-3985-0341-0

Printed and bound by CPI Group (UK) Ltd, Croydon, CR0 4YY

MIX
Paper from
responsible sources
FSC
www.fsc.org
FSC® C171272

For Jet

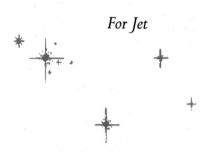

CHAPTER ONE

One of the best things about staying with Nana and Grandad, apart from Grandad's legendary homemade ginger beer and Nana's world-famous apple strudel, was the Hollow Tree. Which was why, as soon as their father had dropped them off for the summer holidays, Lana and Harrison pulled on their wellies, clomped down the street, and squelched their way across the marsh to where their old friend was waiting.

There is something magical about hollow trees. Some people say they are the home of fairies and sprites, and that you should always turn your coat inside out before you climb into one to protect yourself from their spells. Others say they are the entrances to enchanted worlds. Whether you believe in magic or not, if you ever played in the Hollow Tree at Nana and Grandad's house, you would never forget it. It was hollow all the way up the inside, and generations of children had carved handholds so you could climb right up and stick your head out of the top.

Best of all, it seemed to have a face. In the middle of its trunk, two empty eye sockets sat above a twisty nose-hole, below which was a gaping mouth lined with bulges that looked just like grinning teeth. Add to that the fact that its broken branches looked just like hair, and you might have thought the whole tree was about to laugh, or burst into song, or maybe just crunch up your bones, swallow and release a leafy burp.

On this day in particular – a day that turned out to be very unusual indeed – the Hollow Tree had a surprise in store for Lana and Harrison. It had been surrounded by a bright yellow plastic safety barrier and pinned to its bark forehead was a large sign which read:

DANGER!
TREE FELLING IN PROGRESS.

'What?' exclaimed Lana in disbelief. 'You can't be serious!'

'They're going to cut it down,' said Harrison mournfully.

Lana's heart sank. She'd recently had a growth

spurt and was hoping that this holiday she would finally be tall enough to reach between the handholds and make it all the way to the top of the tree.

'That's so unfair!' she protested. 'I'll never get to climb it now.'

'I'm sorry, Lana,' said Harrison sympathetically. 'You were looking forward to that. I feel bad for the tree too. It's been here for ever.'

There was a pause.

'I'm going anyway,' said Lana determinedly.

'No!' said Harrison, catching her by the arm. 'Look at the sign. We're not allowed.'

'But there's no one here!' protested Lana.

'There's no one here *yet*,' corrected Harrison. 'They could come any minute,' he added, anxiously turning to scan the horizon. Which gave Lana the perfect opportunity to duck under the safety barrier.

'Lana!' hissed Harrison, as she hopped across the marsh. 'You'll get us into trouble!'

But Lana was already jumping from tuft to tuft across the marshy field, heading straight for the Hollow Tree.

'Come back!' shouted Harrison, but Lana wasn't listening.

'I'm going in!' she called, squeezing her head and arms through the tree's open mouth. She breathed in the old familiar darkness: a delicious mix of wet leaves, fresh fungus, and dry rotting wood. Wriggling forward until just her legs were poking out, she tumbled inside and landed in an undignified heap in the giant hollow. Then, as she struggled to her feet, a stray twig spiked the top of her head.

'Ow!' she howled, rubbing the sore spot.

'Lana?' called Harrison from behind the barrier. 'Are you okay?'

There is something magical about hollow trees

'No!' she lied. She wasn't really hurt; she just wanted Harrison to join her. Seconds later, he landed heavily beside her.

'Something scratched me,' she sobbed. 'Is it bleeding?'

'Stand in the light a minute.' Lana moved to the centre of the hollow and Harrison made a fingertip search of her hair. 'I can't see anything. Come on, let's go back.'

'No,' Lana said, pulling at his sleeve. 'I want to climb up there.' She pointed to the little blue circle of sky at the top of the Hollow Tree.

'No way,' said Harrison.

Lana stretched herself to her full height, but she couldn't quite reach the first handhold.

'I need a boost,' she begged.

Harrison shook his head and folded his arms. 'What if someone comes while you're up there? It's too dangerous.'

'Please,' begged Lana. 'You've done it. This could be my last chance.'

Harrison gave her one of his Weary Looks. Then he cradled his hands and launched Lana upwards towards the light. But as soon as she gripped a handhold, they heard voices in the distance.

'There's someone coming!' said Harrison anxiously, grabbing Lana's ankle. 'STOP!' he shouted over his shoulder. 'THERE ARE CHILDREN—!'

Lana toppled back on top of him, swiftly untangled herself, then clamped her hand over his mouth. 'They're just talking!' she hissed. 'Look.'

Harrison followed her gaze out of the tree's mouth to where four adults were approaching the yellow fence.

'See?' said Lana. 'No saws or diggers or anything. Just be quiet. Then we won't get in any trouble.'

Harrison nodded his agreement, and when Lana took her hand away, they each moved to one of the eyeholes, listening in on the conversation.

A confident-looking woman with long braids was talking.

'Thank you for coming, everyone,' she said. 'I'm Gudrun Lloyd, the mayor. Carl Ellis is the developer in charge of this project.'

A stocky bald man wearing canvas shorts and a leather waist bag nodded.

'And this is Professor North, our spider expert.'

A tall, slim lady with white hair and a striking gold necklace forced a thin smile. Next to her, a dark-haired man with a patterned red scarf coughed politely, asking for Gudrun's attention.

'Oh! I'm so sorry,' said Gudrun. 'This is Yashar Falarmarzi, the local science teacher who first noticed we had spiders living in the marsh.'

'Thank you, Gudrun,' said Yashar with a winning smile. 'Carl, thank you so much for meeting with us today . . .'

Carl held up a hand to silence Yashar, then turned to Professor North.

'Let's cut to the chase, shall we?' he snapped. 'This project has been years in the planning and will provide seventy-five much-needed high-quality homes.

It has cost me millions of pounds, not to mention years of my life . . .' His voice trailed off and he snatched a breath. 'And you want to cancel it, just because of a few poxy spiders?'

There was a long pause, while Professor North regarded him steadily. 'Not cancel,' she replied coldly. 'Delay.'

'Are you out of your mind?' snarled Carl angrily.

Yashar, the teacher, appeared between them. 'You have to understand, Mr Ellis,' he began in a soothing voice, 'these are no ordinary spiders. They are Golden Diving Bells, and they are extremely rare. So rare that they are on the brink of extinction. All we're asking for is a chance to move them to another location.'

'For a teacher, you're not very bright, are you?' snapped Carl. 'Tell him, Mayor.'

Gudrun sheepishly stared down at her feet. She looked over to the Hollow Tree – and saw movement in its eyes!

'Aaagh!' she screamed.

'What the——!' exclaimed Carl.

'The tree!' shrieked Gudrun, pointing straight at Lana. 'It's alive!'

CHAPTER TWO

'Who's there?' yelled Carl.

'DON'T PANIC!' piped up Harrison, clambering out. 'We're just two kids!'

'Sorry!' blurted Lana, climbing out after him. 'We didn't mean to scare you.'

'Can't you read?' bellowed Carl, pointing to the danger sign.

'They're children,' said Gudrun firmly. She took

a deep breath and gave Lana and Harrison a broad smile. 'So, who do we have here?'

'I'm Lana. And this is my brother Harrison.'

'I've got a son about your age,' said Gudrun. 'He's called Kyle. He plays around here sometimes. Maybe you've met him?'

'Has he climbed the Hollow Tree?' asked Lana.

'So he tells me,' chuckled Gudrun. 'He's very adventurous.' There was kindness in her warm brown eyes, and Lana smiled shyly back at her. 'I'm so sorry,' she continued, 'for shrieking like that. I hope I didn't scare you.' Talking to the children seemed to be relaxing her, and she took a deep breath. 'I have to be honest: all this talk of spiders has me on edge. I keep thinking one's going to leap out at me.'

'You'd never notice if one did,' clipped Professor North, fiddling with her necklace. 'They're tiny.'

'Are they?' asked Gudrun hopefully.

'Let me see if I can find one,' said Professor North, crouching beside one of the many puddles that dotted the marsh and scanning the depths of the water.

'Good luck,' Carl huffed. 'I've not seen so much as a tadpole.'

'Here,' said Professor North, breaking off a stalk of marsh grass, and beckoning Gudrun towards her.

Intrigued, Harrison edged closer, while Lana – who wasn't sure she wanted to meet a spider face to face – held nervously back. Professor North was using the stalk as a pointer, and at its tip was a flash of gold.

'That's a special web called a diving bell that it makes as its home,' she said softly. 'See? No bigger than my little fingernail. And the spider inside is even smaller.'

'But . . .' began Harrison with a look of confusion. 'Spiders don't live underwater.'

'That's what makes the Golden Diving Bell spider so special,' Yashar supplied enthusiastically. 'It spins its home out of silk, then fills it with air.'

'Fascinating,' said Carl, in a bored voice that made clear it absolutely wasn't.

Professor North rolled her eyes, then raised herself to her full height.

'They have to be moved,' she stated bluntly.

'Tell her, Mayor,' said Carl again, looking pointedly at Gudrun.

There was a pause while Gudrun tried to find the right words. 'It's not that simple,' she said awkwardly. 'The works are due to start first thing tomorrow and the council has approved them. A delay will be very expensive.'

'But if we destroy their habitat, these precious

creatures may disappear for ever,' countered Yashar, with feeling.

'Sorry,' Carl snorted, 'but spiders aren't precious. Bees maybe, because they make honey. But spiders don't make anything.'

'They make webs,' added Harrison helpfully.

'Exactly,' broke in Professor North. 'Spiders eat flies. And flies eat crops. Without them, we wouldn't be able to grow food. So . . .' She turned to Mayor Gudrun and looked her right in the eye. 'Are you going to save these spiders, or aren't you?'

'I don't know what to say,' said Gudrun.

'You know what your problem is?' asked Carl, squaring up to Professor North. 'You prefer spiders to people.'

'Just some people,' replied Professor North, staring coolly back at him. Lana stifled a smile.

'Tell you what,' said Carl defiantly. 'Let's ask

the kids. They're the ones that play here, aren't they?' He put his hands on his knees, bringing his face down to Lana's height, and Lana's nose tickled with the scent of aftershave. 'What would you rather? A stinky old marsh full of spiders, or a brand-new adventure playground?'

'An adventure playground?' repeated Lana, feeling a flutter of excitement.

'You betcha,' said Carl.

'Will it have a zip wire?' asked Lana hopefully.

'And a pirate ship,' added Carl. 'And maybe a climbing wall, agreed in principle but subject to best endeavours. So? What do you think?'

'I think we should save the spiders,' said Harrison firmly. Professor North caught his eye and smiled.

'And what about you?' asked Carl, turning to Lana.

'I don't really like spiders,' she said, doing her

best to ignore both Harrison and Professor North's disapproving scowls. 'They give me the creeps. But if you do all this building on the marsh, can we still keep the tree? Everyone round here loves it, and I really want to climb it.'

'Lana,' said Harrison snippily. 'That's really selfish.'

Carl grinned, revealing a large gold tooth. 'Deal,' he said, holding out his hand.

Lana looked apologetically at Harrison. 'In that case . . .' She put her hand in Carl's and shook it. 'I'd like an adventure playground.'

CHAPTER THREE

'Lana? Are you listening?'

Lana jolted back to reality to see Nana sat beside her bed, reading from a storybook. It was one of Lana's favourites – *Beowulf* – about a brave warrior who saves a village from a marauding monster.

'Sorry, Nana.'

'Shall I put the light out?'

'No, please. I'm enjoying it. It's just . . .'

Lana's eyes wandered back to the picture of a wooden village next to a wide blue lake, surrounded by forest, with snow-capped mountains behind it.

'Where is that?' she asked.

Nana chuckled. 'I'm not sure it's a real place, to be honest. But it's very pretty.'

Lana nodded. It looked like the closest thing to a perfect world she could possibly imagine. It should have made her happy, but something was bothering her.

'Nana, do you think it's bad – what they're doing to the spiders?'

'Spiders?' repeated Nana with a puzzled smile. 'What spiders are these?'

'The ones in the marsh,' replied Lana. Her bottom lip began to wobble.

'Is everything all right, love?' asked Nana, concerned.

Lana felt a wave of emotion rise inside her, and before she knew quite what was happening, she was burying her face in Nana's shoulder, and heaving with sobs.

'Hey, hey, Lana,' said Nana gently. 'What's the matter?'

'They're going to kill the spiders,' said Lana, pulling away. 'And it's all my fault.'

Nana put a soothing hand on her back.

'You're not explaining this very well, darling. Who's "they"?'

'The people building the houses.' Lana gulped.

'I see,' said Nana, catching up. 'Is this about the new housing estate over in the fields?'

Lana nodded.

'The builder asked me if I wanted to save the spiders and I said no. So now they're going to go extinct and Harrison's angry with me.' Lana dissolved into tears again. 'I'm a bad person!'

'Shush, now, shush.' Nana held her tight, rocking her back and forth. 'You made a mistake, that's all. In the heat of the moment. I'm sure if you explain that to Harrison, he'll understand.'

Nana brushed the tears from Lana's cheeks, kissed the top of her head, and ran her fingers through her tangled blonde hair to straighten it.

'That's better,' she said.

There was a soft knock, and Grandad peeped round the door. 'Everything okay?'

Lana nodded, smiling through her tears. If she was sad, Grandad always found a way to cheer her up.

'I've got a special treat here,' he announced with a twinkle in his eye. 'But it's only for granddaughters. Any takers?'

'Yes, please, Grandad,' said Lana expectantly.

23

Grandad stepped inside, holding something behind his back.

'Then you need to answer this question,' smiled Grandad, who loved a riddle. 'I am a drink that is made when you're cold. Add some marshmallows to turn me to gold.'

Lana frowned. 'Gold? There aren't any drinks that turn to gold.'

'Hot chocolate!' said Grandad, holding up a steaming mug.

'But that doesn't turn to gold,' said Lana, wrinkling her nose.

'Gold as in *precious*,' said Grandad. 'I'd better test it first, though, before I give it to you. Just in case it's not up to standard.' He took a cheeky sip of the frothy hot chocolate.

'Oi!' said Lana, enjoying the game. 'Stop it!'

'Seems okay to me,' said Grandad, with a solemn

look. 'But I'd better make sure,' he continued,

taking another sip.

'Oh, Mick,' said Nana. 'Give it to her.'

'So, what was all the fuss about?' asked Grandad,

handing her the mug at last.

'Lana and Harrison met the builders, I think.

When they were playing by the Hollow Tree,'

said Nana.

Lana nodded. 'He said he's a developer. Called Carl. And he wants to build houses on the marsh. He asked me which I preferred, spiders or an adventure playground.' She sniffed. 'And I said—'

'An adventure playground,' finished Grandad. 'What kid wouldn't?'

'Harrison,' replied Lana. 'He said we should save the spiders.'

'Spiders?' echoed Grandad, puzzled. 'Wait a minute . . .' His face clouded. 'I saw something about this earlier.'

Lana and Nana shared a look while Grandad tapped at his phone. News was one of Grandad's obsessions.

'Found it,' he said, peering at the screen. 'Mayor Gudrun Lloyd will host an eleventh-hour crisis meeting today between local developer Carl Ellis and spider expert Professor Araminta

North, known in conservationist circles as "the Spider Queen". Building work on local marshland is due to begin tomorrow, but there are concerns over a colony of rare spiders. Yashar Falarmarzi, the science teacher who first discovered the spiders, said, "We appreciate that there are costs involved, but we have to move the spiders to a new habitat. The mayor has the power to delay the project, and I really hope she uses it. We can't let these beautiful creatures be wiped out.'"

'That's them!' exclaimed Lana, scrolling through a series of photographs beneath the article. 'And look, that's one of the spiders!'

'So why are they still building?' asked Nana. 'If the spiders are protected?'

Grandad marched to the window, yanked back the curtain, and peered out.

'I can see lights down there,' he said grimly. 'I'm going to take a look.'

Moments later, he was back, the jolly twinkle in his eye completely gone.

'It's true,' he said, shaking his head in disbelief. 'All sorts of stuff's arriving: diggers, trucks, the lot. They must be going ahead.'

'Surely they can't?' asked Nana. 'Not if they found a rare species.'

Grandad shrugged. 'I guess they can,' he said.

Long after Nana and Grandad had turned out her light, Lana lay awake, snippets of the afternoon's conversation playing in her mind.

It was still light outside, making her feel restless, and she rolled over onto her side, trying to get comfortable. But her neck itched, her mouth was dry, and her legs felt like they belonged to someone else.

She heard Harrison creaking up the stairs, and the sound of the tap running as he cleaned his teeth. Then Nana and Grandad wishing him goodnight.

His door closed, and the TV was switched on downstairs.

It's my fault, she told herself, her insides tight with guilt. *They're going to fill in the marsh and kill the spiders, and it's all my fault.*

She rolled over onto her other side, unable to find any position that wasn't too hot, too cold, too firm, or too soft. *What was it Mum always said when she couldn't sleep?* 'Just lie still with your eyes closed and think of nice things.'

She took a deep breath, then another, then another. Little by little, she felt her body melt into the mattress, until at long last, there it was: a teeny-tiny sleepy feeling. All she needed to do was float towards it . . .

Something was tugging at her finger.

The room was dark. Opening her eyes, Lana looked at the glowing clock on her bedside table. Midnight. Switching on her lamp, she held her hand up to her face. Wound around her index finger, running all the way to the open door, was a thin golden thread, glimmering in the lamplight.

And something, somewhere, was pulling on it.

CHAPTER FOUR

'Harrison?' Lana hissed, peering into the darkness beyond the doorway. 'Is that you?'

Once again, the thread pulled faintly at her finger. Lana frowned. It had to be her brother, playing a trick on her. Probably to get her back for the spiders.

She called softly, 'Harrison!'

But there was no answer.

With a sigh of frustration, she threw back the covers, got up and yanked open the bedroom door, fully expecting to see her brother's grinning face behind it. But the landing was empty.

He must be in his room, she thought. *Crouching behind the door, tugging on the thread, trying his hardest not to giggle. Well, unlucky, Harrison!* she gloated silently, creeping across the landing and throwing open the door of his bedroom. *You're about to get caught!*

But Harrison was tucked up in bed, fast asleep.

Lana frowned as the thread twitched again. If Harrison wasn't pulling it, who was? Grandad, maybe?

Confused, she clicked open the door to Nana and Grandad's room. But Nana was fast asleep with her eye mask on and Grandad was snoring loudly, so she quietly pulled it shut again.

33

Tug-tug-tug. Her eyes were adjusting, and she could now see the thread, glimmering in the darkness, stretching all the way from her finger to the top of the stairs.

Lana's heart began to race. Pulling gently on the thread, she crossed back to her bedroom and unhooked her unicorn dressing gown from the peg on the back of the door. Getting her arms in the sleeves wasn't easy, because the thread seemed to be sticky. Peeling it away from her finger, it stuck to her elbow, then the belt of her dressing gown, before somehow attaching itself to the end of her nose. Eventually she untangled herself and was back in her brother's room, dressing gown retied, and the thread once again wrapped around her finger.

'Harrison! Wake up!'

Her brother grunted and rolled over.

'Harrison, help!'

He sat up in bed and scowled.

'Lana, *sssh*!' he growled. 'Why do you have to be so annoying all the time? I'm trying to sleep!'

'I'm serious!' squeaked Lana. 'There's something stuck to the end of my finger!'

Harrison shook his head in disbelief, then reluctantly clambered out of bed.

'No, there isn't,' he said, waving his hand in front of Lana. 'See? Nothing there.'

Except of course, there was.

'Eww!' He winced as his wrist got stuck on the golden thread. 'What *is* that?'

'Some weird thread,' blurted Lana. 'I woke up with it on my finger! And there's something on the other end of it. Feel!'

Harrison pinched the thread between his finger and thumb, his eyes widening in surprise as whatever was on the other end began to pull back in a series of short, sharp movements.

'See?' asked Lana. 'I told you!'

'Maybe I should wake up Nana and Grandad,' said Harrison thoughtfully.

'What?' asked Lana, eyes shining. 'And ruin the adventure?'

She could see Harrison was tempted.

'They'll just tell us to go back to bed,' she urged. 'And we'll never find out where it goes.'

After a pause, while Harrison's daring and not-so-daring sides battled it out, he said in a hushed voice, 'Come on, then.'

Quiet as mice, the two of them tiptoed down the stairs, Lana winding the thread around her wrist as they went.

'Look,' said Harrison breathlessly as they reached the hallway. A full moon rippled in the frosted glass of the front door. 'It's leading outside. We need to put our boots on.'

They'd barely taken two steps down the path when the golden thread tugged again, hurrying them through the front gate and out onto the close. Lana could see a thin golden line glittering in front of her, leading all the way from the loop on her finger to the gate that opened onto the marsh. Either side of it stood two giant diggers. Framed between them was their old playmate, its broken branches silhouetted against the moon.

'Of course!' exclaimed Harrison. 'It's taking us to the Hollow Tree! Come on!'

Navigating the marsh was tricky at the best of times, but it was almost impossible in the dark, with a golden thread wrapped around your finger. Both children slipped more than once, and by the time they reached the tree, Harrison's boots were sloshing with water and Lana's right hand was covered in stinky marsh-mud.

The thread led directly into the mouth of the tree, so Lana squeezed through headfirst. Moments later, Harrison came tumbling in after her.

The thread went slack, and for a few seconds they lay on their backs in the dark, panting.

Once again, the thread began to twitch, tugging insistently, making Lana scramble to her feet.

'Harrison . . .' she said quietly. 'It wants me to climb.'

CHAPTER FIVE

For several moments, Lana and Harrison stood in the darkness of the hollow, staring upwards at the glimmering thread, their faces lit by stray moonbeams. 'Harrison, I need your help.'

Harrison looked at her doubtfully. 'Are you sure you're tall enough? What happens if you get stuck?'

'I won't.' Lana shrugged.

'Or worse,' continued Harrison, nodding in the

direction of the thread. 'What if there's something really scary on the other end of that thing?'

Harrison,' said Lana, pulling a face. 'Don't be so negative – this is exciting! Now, come on, give me a boost.'

Harrison shook his head. 'Okay,' he said wearily. 'But I'm coming with you.'

Cradling his hands, he lifted Lana up. After a moment of scrabbling, she reached a handhold and began to climb.

'Harrison!' she crowed. 'I'm doing it, look! I'm finally climbing the Hollow Tree!'

Working her way slowly up the inside of the trunk, listening to the sound of her own breath, Lana felt full of possibility and freedom.

Below her, Harrison shifted uneasily.

'DON'T FALL!' he called, his voice echoing around her. 'OR YOU'LL SQUISH ME!'

But Lana had no intention of falling. She was nearly at the top and determined to see who – or what – was controlling the thread.

'Almost there!' she called.

'CAN YOU SPEAK A BIT MORE QUIETLY?' boomed Harrison. 'THE TREE MAKES YOUR VOICE REALLY LOUD. IT'S LIKE BEING INSIDE A TRUMPET.'

But Lana didn't reply because she was too busy pulling herself up into what looked like a totally different universe!

The change was so striking that for a moment she couldn't take it in.

Down on the marsh the sky had been still and silent. Up here, however, a sharp wind was blowing and the moon was just a dull glow behind banks of wild-looking cloud. Looking out, Lana saw to her amazement that the Hollow Tree now stood in a snow-covered clearing at the foot of a small basin-shaped valley, surrounded by snow-caked fir trees. What's more, its broken stumps of branches had disappeared. In their place were elegant boughs, their leaves glittering with ice crystals, feathering down to a carpet of deep snow!

'Harrison!' she called. 'You have to see this!'

'TOO LOUD!' came the reply.

'Sorry!' hissed Lana.

Moments later, her brother hauled himself up beside her. 'Wow!' he said, catching his breath. 'Where are we?'

'I have no clue,' replied Lana, holding up the golden thread. 'But this thing's still pulling!'

'Over there!' whispered Harrison, pointing to a clump of trees at the edge of the forest. 'Something moved!'

The distant trees were swaying and shaking, gobbets of snow tumbling from their branches.

Lana looked down at the thread and shivered with foreboding.

'Harrison . . .' she said slowly. 'I think whatever's calling me is coming from in there.'

The thread yanked hard, and Lana found herself stumbling out onto one of the branches.

'I'm going to fall!' she yelled, fighting to stay upright.

'Jump!' bellowed Harrison.

'I can't!' squeaked Lana, glancing down, terrified. The snow beneath her looked very far away indeed. 'It's too high!'

'You've got no choice!' urged Harrison. 'Get as far down the branch as you can, then hang down and let go!'

Lana did as she was told, steadying herself with

handfuls of twigs as she sidestepped swiftly down the branch.

But the thread had other ideas. It yanked her off the branch and out into thin air!

'AAAARGH!' she bellowed. 'Harrison, help me!'

The snow rushed up to greet her, and she braced herself, ready for impact. But as she landed, she kept moving! The snow surged up over her feet, past her waist, then right over the top of her head!

Everything went silent.

Lana opened her eyes to find herself wedged deep in a snowdrift. 'Harrison!' she bawled, trying to struggle free, but it was like shouting into a pillow.

She felt a flush of panic – was she trapped? – then the thread began to pull with greater force than ever, yanking her upwards by the wrist.

Lana's head broke the surface and she found herself gliding across the snow on her front like a human toboggan, heading straight for the swaying clump of trees. A shadow moved in the branches above, and a figure leaped towards her!

Oof! Something had grabbed her leg!

Hardly daring to look, Lana glanced behind her to see Harrison hanging on to her right boot, hitching a ride through the snowdrift.

'I'm not leaving you!' he yelled.

'What do we do now?' yelped Lana, as the two of them bumped rapidly over the snow.

'Hope whatever's pulling us isn't hungry!' bawled Harrison.

The thread went slack, and they slid to a halt on the edge of the forest, hearts racing. From within the trees came the crack and swish of branches, and the thread around Lana's finger began to twitch as a gut-wrenching scream pierced the air.

'What was that?' stammered Harrison, frightened.

Lana shook her head. 'An animal. And it sounds like it's in pain.'

She bit her lip, wrestling with her conscience. Lana wanted to run, to put as much distance as she possibly could between her and whatever creature was thrashing around in the undergrowth. But another part of her knew that wouldn't be right.

She took a deep breath and pushed herself to her feet. 'Where are you going?' asked Harrison, eyes wide.

'To see if it needs help,' Lana replied. Heart thumping in her chest, she pushed through the clump of twitching firs, into the heart of the forest.

Something enormous and white flashed amid the greenery, stopping her in her tracks. Fear gripped her, mouth dry as dust.

Were those hooves? Was that a tail? It couldn't be . . . could it?

It was. With something between a roar and a bray, a gargantuan snow-white beast reared into view, eyes wild, mane flowing, pawing the air with hooves the size of dinner plates. Corkscrewing out from the middle of its forehead, circled with golden thread, was a single, deadly sharp, pitch-black horn.

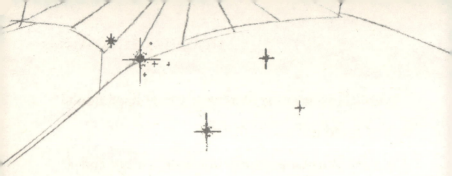

CHAPTER SIX

'Harrison! Come quick!'

Lana's brother pushed his way through snow-sodden branches, his mouth falling open in surprise.

'It's a unicorn!' gasped Lana. 'The thread is tied to his horn!'

As she spoke, the frightened animal tried to run towards them, but razor-thin strands of gold tightened across his chest. In his panic, he had been circling among the trees, the golden thread trapping him like a fly in a web.

'He's trying to get loose! But wait . . .' Harrison's face clouded, as he glanced back towards the Hollow Tree. 'Who tied him to you?'

Lana shrugged. 'Whoever they are, they're not a very nice person. He's terrified, look.'

As if he could hear her, the unicorn shook his head and let out a heart-rending whinny. 'I'm going to get that thread off his horn,' said Lana, stepping forward, determined.

The unicorn brayed in alarm, twisting and turning in the narrow space between the glittering threads.

'Careful,' cautioned Harrison. 'You're scaring him.'

Lana took another step, smiling, hoping the unicorn couldn't hear her heart thumping.

'It's a unicorn! The thread is tied to his horn!'

'Don't be scared,' she soothed, inching closer. 'We want to help you.'

The unicorn backed up, nostrils flaring, his tail accidentally catching the threads behind him and sticking to them like flypaper. Terrified, he lunged forward, only to get caught again as more threads crisscrossed his chest.

Lana held herself sure and steady. '*Sssh*,' she whispered. 'Don't be scared.'

The unicorn held his head to one side, watching her warily. 'Here,' soothed Lana, reaching out her hand.

The unicorn stepped backwards, still eyeing her suspiciously.

Lana inhaled softly and blew through her lips, trying to sound like a horse. It seemed to work because the unicorn whinnied again in reply!

'Good boy,' said Lana softly, reaching to where

the thread was wrapped around the poor creature's horn. But the instant her fingers met the thread, they seemed to stick fast!

'What's the matter?' asked Harrison, seeing her distress.

'Help!' said Lana. 'I'm stuck!'

But the unicorn was backing up, pulling Lana quickly into the web!

'Help!' she yelled, trying to wriggle free. But it was no use: the more she struggled, the more the golden strands stuck fast. Then, out of nowhere, a wild blizzard howled around her, blocking everything from view.

'Lana!' called Harrison, from somewhere within the snowstorm. 'What's happening?'

Before Lana could answer, there was a shift in the wind, and instead of the unicorn, she found herself face to face with a tall, white-haired woman in a long golden cloak and a bright gold necklace. Lana gasped with recognition. It was Professor North, the spider expert from that afternoon!

'Lana,' said the woman, her dark eyes glinting. 'So glad you could join me.'

'It-it's YOU!' stammered Lana. 'The spider lady! What are you doing here?'

'Teaching you a lesson!' bellowed Professor North, towering over her. Touching her gold necklace, she laughed manically as lightning forked in the sky. 'Come,' she smirked, extending a bony hand. Heart in her throat, Lana tried to pull free of the web as her brother came barrelling through the storm, colliding with Professor North and knocking her flat!

'Run, Lana!' called Harrison breathlessly. 'Run!'

But Lana was stuck fast.

For a split second, the driving snow cleared, and she glimpsed Professor North struggling to her feet.

Thinking quickly, Lana undid the belt around her waist and slipped out of her dressing gown, leaving it gummed to the web. Her heart pounding, she crawled, scurried and scrambled away as fast as her legs would carry her.

'Lana!'

It was Harrison's voice, but it now seemed much farther away.

'Harrison!' she yelled, as the wind swirled around her. 'Harrison!'

Everywhere she looked, she saw nothing but white. Then once again, the wind shifted, and for the briefest of moments, she glimpsed her brother through the snow. The dark figure of

Professor North was holding him firmly by the wrist.

Then the blizzard raged again, wiping them from view.

CHAPTER SEVEN

'Harrison!' cried Lana, panic rising in her throat. 'Harrison!'

But there was no answer. She stumbled through the wind, arms outstretched, but all that greeted her was driving snow.

'Harrison!'

It was useless. She put her hands on her knees, fighting for breath.

Then, as suddenly as they had arrived, the

snowflakes departed, chasing each other up into the threatening sky.

She was alone. Harrison and Professor North had vanished. All that remained was her dressing gown, fluttering in the breeze, glued fast to the shimmering web of golden thread.

'Harrison!' she called again.

She rubbed her shoulders, as much to comfort herself as to try and keep warm. Her brother had been taken by the spider lady, she felt sure of it. But where? And why? There was no doubt in her mind: she had to find him. Glancing down, she saw the golden thread, still stuck to her finger. An anxious thought struck her: it was clearly magic, and what if she couldn't undo herself from it? *I mustn't panic*, she thought. *I mustn't panic*. Trapping the trailing end with her foot, she turned her finger round and round, breathing steadily, unwinding the sticky fibre from her wrist, then her finger, until suddenly she was free.

Heaving a sigh of relief, Lana searched the surrounding snow for tracks, but she found nothing. Which way had they gone? Scurrying back through the snow-caked trees to the clearing, she scanned the empty horizon. She was beginning to lose all hope when the sharp sound of a hunting horn rang out, echoing through the forest.

Lana held her breath, listening hard. There it was again: one long stabbing note, drifting down through the trees.

Without a second thought, she ran up the slope of the valley towards it. Hunting horns meant hunters. Maybe they could help her find Harrison.

PEEARP-UP-UP-UP-ARP!

Soon Lana was trudging between the silent evergreens, with nothing but the sound of the horn to guide her. *Where am I?* she wondered, both scared and amazed by the magic she'd just witnessed. The ground steepened, and she found herself climbing up between giant snow-dusted boulders onto a large flat rock. The far side ended sharply in a precipice! Lana shuffled forward on all fours, and a familiar landscape rose into view.

She was kneeling at the edge of an enormous canyon, whose sides were cloaked in dense green forest. A sharp breeze was blowing, and in the far distance were the jagged peaks of enormous, snow-capped mountains. At their foot flashed a wide lake, so large it might be an ocean. A row of tiny geometric shapes caught her eye, and her heart leaped. A jumble of wooden houses stood on the lake shore. It was just like the picture of the village in her storybook! *Could that be where the Spider Lady had taken Harrison?*

It was just like the picture in her storybook!

PEEARP-UP-UP-UP-ARP-UP-UP!

There was the horn again. It sounded like it was coming from the trees at the bottom of the canyon. She needed to find a way down there, fast. But how?

Lana paused, searching for a solution. If only that chattering water would shut up and let her concentrate . . .

Of course – running water! Hadn't Harrison once told her that streams merge into rivers that then flow into lakes? If she followed the water down the hillside, maybe it would lead her all the way to the houses she could see on the shore.

A well-worn animal path led her quickly through the maze of boulders to a tiny pool, its far edge brimming over to form the top of a miniature waterfall. Lana edged down the neighbouring rock, following the narrow strip of babbling water as it splashed its way down the steep hillside, sure that every slip and slide was bringing her closer to her brother.

As it reached the forest, the stream began to widen, and she found herself jogging excitedly along its pebble-strewn bank, through clumps of brightly coloured wildflowers.

The sound of the horn was growing closer. And could she hear dogs barking?

Lana froze, breathing hard. Then suddenly an enormous brown bear came lumbering round the bend, sending arcs of spray from the stream high into the air!

CHAPTER EIGHT

Lana's body surged with energy, and she turned to run, blood thumping in her ears.

'Wait!'

Was she imagining things, or had a bear just shouted at her? Lana slowed down and turned round.

'Tell them I went that way!' instructed the bear as he bolted up the bank, springing up the trunk of the nearest pine tree as easily as if it were a ladder. Swiftly reaching the top, he froze, stock still, hidden among the upper branches.

Lana frowned. The bear was wearing a red scarf round his neck. Its bright pattern looked very familiar.

PEEARP-UP-UP-UP-ARP!

Lana swallowed hard. She turned just in time to see a huge pack of hounds sprint round the bend, baying and kicking up water as they went.

Quick as a flash, she clambered up the lower branches of the same pine the bear had scaled, as the dogs surged up the bank, breaking like a wave around the base of the tree. Close up, they were terrifying: a bubbling mass of bloodshot eyes, snarling teeth and lashing tails!

The piercing sound of the horn blasted again,

and four riders came racing up.

'Did a bear come this way?!' rasped the leader. He was dressed in furs, like a character from her story, *Beowulf*, with a dark leather skull cap on his head. His horse, a colossal beast with a chestnut coat, began to twist and turn in the stream, eager for the chase. Behind him rode two men and a woman dressed in woollen tunics. Moonlight flashed on their spears.

'Don't be afraid,' the man said with a slow smile, and one of his teeth flashed gold. 'We mean you no harm.'

Lana had seen that grin before. It was Carl Ellis, the developer she'd made a deal with!

'Hey!' called Lana, trying to make herself heard above the hounds. 'It's me, Lana.'

'Girl, I know you not. We're looking for a talking bear.'

'I met you earlier today – you promised me an adventure playground!' insisted Lana, trying to jog his memory.

'The bear!' demanded Carl. 'Did you see him? You didn't speak to him, I hope? He's highly dangerous.'

'He went that way!' shouted Lana, pointing across the stream.

'Yah!' bellowed Carl, cracking his whip at the dogs, who began to gather around him. 'Come down from that tree and get yourself to the village,' he shouted. 'It's not safe out here!'

'Yes, Carl,' replied Lana loudly, puzzled as to why he didn't recognize her.

'Sire!' exclaimed the female guard. 'She knows your name!'

'It's Warden to you, young scamp,' he sneered, narrowing his eyes at Lana. Then with a final blast on the horn, he and his three guards went charging across the stream and into the forest.

'Have they gone?' called the bear from further up in the tree.

'Gone!' Lana confirmed, climbing carefully back down to the ground.

The upper branches of the tree began to rustle, and the bear lowered himself into view. Lana made a mental note that if she ever came across a dangerous bear, there was no point trying to climb to safety.

'Thanks,' he called. 'And if you ever need any help . . .'

Lana's eyes widened expectantly.

'. . . find some other bear to do it,' he snapped, clambering back up into the treetop. 'That was far too close for comfort.'

'But I do need help!' called Lana. 'I've lost my brother!'

'I'm leaving now!' called the bear, hurling his weight from side to side so that the upper branches of the pine rocked back and forth, then leaping to the neighbouring tree.

'He's been kidnapped!'

The bear glanced down at her, briefly curious, as he swayed in the canopy. Then he shook his head, deciding to ignore her.

'Sorry,' he called, leaping to the next treetop. 'Not my problem.'

Lana burned with anger. She had risked her life to save him, and now he was ignoring her!

'Fine!' she called, trotting along the ground beneath him. 'I'll call the hunters back.' The bear, swaying in the upper branches, prepared his next jump.

'Hallo!' called Lana, turning in the direction the hunters had gone. 'You know that bear you're looking for? He's over here!'

The bear paused in the treetop, allowing the branches to settle. He sniffed the air, as if making sure the hunters were a safe distance away. Then, as easily as if he was using a hotel lift, he slid all the way down the tree until he was standing right next to Lana.

'Fine,' he said. 'Have it your own way.'

He started towards her, and Lana flinched in fear. But instead, the bear offered her a genteel paw.

'I was going to give you a ride,' he explained. 'May I?'

Lana nodded nervously, and the bear swept her up on his shoulders.

'Grab onto my neckerchief!' he called and together they went rocketing back up the tree and into the leafy canopy.

CHAPTER NINE

Soon Lana and the bear were flying through the treetops, leaving the hunters way behind them. Once again, Lana glimpsed the lake, shimmering in the moonlight, and the dark huts beside it. She was about to ask the bear if that might be where Professor North had taken Harrison, when he crashed to a halt, swinging in the branches.

'*Sssh*!' he whispered. 'You see that nest?'

Lana followed his gaze.

'There's a red kite in there, sitting on eggs.' A large bird with a forked tail circled into view, a writhing snake gripped in its enormous talons.

'That's the father,' explained the bear. 'He's about to serve a midnight snack. Come on, let's not disturb them.' He sniffed deeply before plunging downwards.

A few seconds later the bear let go of the lowest branch, and they dropped onto the forest floor, Lana gripping his neckerchief tight so as not to fall off.

'What about the dogs?' asked Lana.

'What about them?' replied the bear over his shoulder.

'Isn't that why you swing through the trees, so you don't leave a scent?'

The bear grunted, impressed.

'Precisely so,' he replied. 'But that kite lives right above my cave, and I'm not disturbing him.'

They had reached a large bank of gorse bushes. The bear raised himself up onto his hind legs and turned full circle, snuffling in the air. To Lana, sitting on his shoulders, his wet nostrils seemed as wide and powerful as a vacuum-cleaner nozzle.

'We're good,' he said confidently, swooping Lana to the ground.

Happy that they hadn't been followed, the bear went over to two thorn-laden bushes and pulled their brambles apart. Standing aside like a doorman outside an expensive hotel, he gestured to Lana.

'After you.'

The thorns on the bushes were the size of knitting needles, and Lana edged warily through the gap. She found herself standing at the foot of a low bank, beside the entrance of a cave.

'Please,' said the bear, stretching out an inviting paw. 'Be my guest.'

Lana wavered, not sure that this was a good idea. 'Is this safe?' she asked, looking the bear right in the eye.

'Nothing here is safe,' countered the bear. 'Now please go inside.'

Lana dropped to her hands and knees and shuffled forward into the low archway.

'Keep going,' prompted the bear. After a few moments of crawling, the bear squeezing through the narrow gap behind her, the pine needles beneath Lana's hands turned to cold sand, then to something that felt like matting. 'Just a little further,' urged the bear, 'and you should be able to stand up.'

Lana raised her hands above her head, feeling for the roof of the tunnel. The air smelled of earth and tree roots, reminding her of the familiar soft fug of the Hollow Tree. Sniffing again, she caught fresh fish, too.

'One second,' said the bear. 'Let's shed a little light on the subject, shall we?'

There was the sound of two hard objects being struck together, and a tuft of dried grass burst suddenly into flame, lighting up the bear's face in the darkness. A torch was lit, and then another, and objects began to loom out of the darkness.

There was a small wooden table crowded with brightly coloured glass flasks, some of which looked large enough to boil children in. 'W-what are those?' stammered Lana, worried.

'My potions,' said the bear simply.

'What sort of potions?' asked Lana warily.

A torch was lit and objects began to loom out of the darkness

'Never you mind. Now then,' said the bear, brushing himself down. 'My name is King Yashar of—'

'Yashar?' interrupted Lana. 'I thought you looked familiar!' Now she knew where she had seen those twinkly green eyes and that neckerchief before! 'You're the science teacher!'

'Science teacher?' asked the bear, mystified.

'The one that found the spiders!'

King Yashar stared at her blankly.

'Doesn't matter,' said Lana. She was realizing that everyone in this strange place looked exactly like someone she knew. 'I'm Lana, and I'm looking for my brother, Harrison. We come from a place . . . from somewhere else. I woke up with a golden thread stuck to my finger, which led us here through the Hollow Tree. When we got here, it was attached to a unicorn, which then turned into—'

'A tall woman with white hair?'

Lana started in surprise.

'Exactly! Professor North!'

The bear frowned and lowered his eyes. When he spoke again, his voice was full of frightened awe.

'We call her the Spider Queen.'

Lana's mind flashed back to Grandad and the article in the newspaper. The Spider Queen: wasn't that what they had called her too?

'That's her!' she exclaimed. 'Where has she taken him?'

But instead of answering her question, the bear picked up a grey shell from a nearby bucket and opened it with his teeth.

'Hungry?' he asked. 'How do you feel about oysters?'

Lana glanced down at the watery-looking shellfish sitting on the shiny white half-shell in front of her and grimaced. It looked like something a giantess might find in her handkerchief after blowing her nose.

'No, thank you,' snapped Lana. 'Please answer me. Who exactly is this Spider Queen, and where has she taken my brother?'

The bear snorted, as if she had said something very funny, and reached for a napkin.

'What?' Lana prodded.

The bear looked at her with his head on one side, sizing her up. Whether he was considering her story or working out whether she might make a good side-dish, Lana wasn't quite sure. He tipped back another oyster, swallowed it, and licked his lips.

'Tell me,' said the bear, with a serious look in

his eye. 'Who is it that likes unicorns? You or your brother – Harrison, was it?'

'Me, I guess,' Lana replied.

'Then it's you she wants. The question is, why?'

Lana felt a pang of guilt about the spiders in the marsh, but quickly pushed it away. 'Well, *I* don't know,' she said indignantly.

The bear raised his eyebrows.

'I think I was bad to some spiders,' said Lana guiltily. 'Back home.' Then, after a pause, she added, 'The Spider Queen said she was going to teach me a lesson. But Harrison pushed her and I got away.'

'And that was when he disappeared?'

Lana nodded.

'Then it's simple. She's taken him instead of you. To her palace, no doubt.'

'And where's that?'

'No one knows. I've scoured every inch of this valley, and the valleys beyond, and found nothing.'

'You're searching for her too? Why?'

The bear gazed at her intensely, as if deciding whether to share an important secret.

'I haven't always been a bear. I was born human.' He looked at Lana with steady eyes, studying her reaction. She nodded expectantly. 'You believe me?'

'Of course,' said Lana. 'What happened? Did someone put a spell on you?'

'Yes.' He nodded. 'The Spider Queen.'

'But why? Tell me, please. It might help me find Harrison.'

'Very well,' said the bear grudgingly, putting down the empty shell. 'But don't get your hopes up. The story I'm about to tell you does not end well.' He cleared his throat, ready to begin.

CHAPTER TEN

he land where I grew up is a desolate place, full of blasted heaths, rotting marshes and trees as bare as skeletons. There are few animals to hunt, no fish to catch, and the earth is so poor that the only thing to grow well is moss.

With so little food to go around, my people were always fighting with our neighbours, and we all grew up to become warriors. Whenever there was a moment of peace - which wasn't very often - we dreamed of finding a new home, but none of us ever had the courage to leave.

During one particularly harsh winter, we found ourselves at war with the fiercest of our neighbouring kingdoms. My people triumphed, but four of my seven brothers were killed, along with our father. As the oldest, I became king.

When the snows finally melted, my younger brother Zephir decided he would leave and try to find a new home. News eventually reached us by letter that he had found a glorious new land across the ocean, where the forests were green, the water was pure and the fish were plentiful.

Come and join us, brother! his letter said. This land has everything anyone could ever wish for. It's the perfect place to raise a family and live a peaceful life. Our fishermen work only a few hours in the morning, hauling nets from the jetty, and we have enough oysters to eat for a week! Our evenings are spent in the Great Hall where there is a bed for everyone, and music and singing late into the evening.

He included instructions and a map which covered many miles, but of course, it was impossible for me to go. I was now the leader of my people, and I had a responsibility to see them through hard times. I wrote to Zephir and told him that all of us wished him well, and that maybe, one day, if my brother Mawhad was willing, I might leave him in charge of our kingdom and pay Zephir a visit.

Years passed, and things grew a little easier for us in my country. We had some milder winters, food was more plentiful, and we made peace with our neighbours. My thoughts turned once more to visiting Zephir, when I was shocked to receive a second letter, written in a different hand.

Dear Yashar

Excuse me for writing to you, but I have no one left to turn to. My name is Gudrun—

Wait a minute,' interrupted Lana. 'Did you say Gudrun?'

Yes,' said the bear patiently.

'Has she got braids in her hair?'

The bear looked at her strangely. 'You've met her?'

'Doesn't matter,' said Lana. 'Carry on.'

'Thank you,' said the bear. 'I will.'

My name is Gudrun, and I am your brother Zephir's wife.

I am sorry to tell you that ill fortune has fallen on our village. First came the storms; terrible storms that destroy our boats and batter our homes.

Then came the Beast.

For months now, it has terrorized our village. We built a stockade to try and keep it out, but every night it carries one of our brave warriors away from the Great Hall. We used to be forty strong; now there are barely two dozen of us left.

Last night, your brother Zephir took his turn, waiting up in the Great Hall with his sword and shield, determined to catch and kill the Beast. But this morning, he was gone, his armaments lying untouched on the floor beside his bed.

Come and help us, please. Zephir has spoken of you often and I know you are a great warrior. Maybe you can save us from this dreadful creature and return my husband to me?

Your trusting sister, Gudrun

I needed no further encouragement. I left Mawhad in charge of our people, and marched to the coast, accompanied by twenty of our bravest warriors and a dozen of our finest craftspeople. We built a longship in barely four days, and set sail according to my brother's instructions, but just after we sighted land, there was a terrible storm, and we were shipwrecked.

I alone survived, by clinging to our broken mast, and woke on the shore the next morning, with the tide washing my feet, lucky to be alive.

Several days' march later, I arrived at Zephir's village. In the days since Gudrun had sent her letter, things had got worse. The Great Hall, where there had once been so much joy and merrymaking, was empty: no villagers dared to spend the night there for fear of the mysterious beast.

Determined to face the creature, I bedded down in the Great Hall. Or at least, I pretended to. I kept my eyes half open, and under the sheepskins, I held my trusty sword.

It had never failed me in battle and I was sure I could depend on it now. But nothing came.

For what felt like hours I lay there in the darkness. Eventually, my travels caught up with me. My eyelids weighed heavy and I fell into a deep sleep.

When I awoke, I was lying on golden silk sheets in an enormous gold palace, bound in gold thread, with a strange white-haired woman towering over me!

'That's her!' squeaked Lana. 'The Spider Queen.'

'Please don't interrupt,' replied the bear, startled out of his story. 'Now where was I?'

'In bed, with her towering over you,' prompted Lana.

'Yes, of course.' The bear nodded. 'Thank you.'

'Greetings, O King,' she spat. 'Come to save your brother and his battalion, have you?'

I struggled against my bonds but it was no use. My arms and legs were stuck fast, like a silkworm in a cocoon!

'You've failed,' she gloated. 'They are all trussed up in my larder.'

'Evil woman!' I howled. 'Let them go!'

'What?' she asked. 'And let them harm more of my precious kind?'

I told her I had no idea what she was talking about. She explained that my brother had destroyed her subjects' homes. To begin with, I thought she was crazy. But then, as she ranted and raved, I began to understand: the subjects she ruled over were spiders. They lived in the shallows beside the village, and their webs had been destroyed by the villagers' oyster nets.'

'Golden Diving Bells,' said Lana, knowingly.

'The Spider Queen proposed,' continued the

bear, 'to let me go free on one condition.'

'And what was that?'

'That I banished my brother Zephir and his people from the lake. Of course, there was no way I could agree. When I said as much, she lit up with rage! Snatching up my hand, she bit into my skin, and I fell fast asleep once again.

When I awoke, I was back in the Great Hall. But to my horror, my hands were transformed into giant paws, my body was matted with fur and my enormous teeth felt like boulders beneath my slobbering tongue. I had become a bear! The villagers were banging on the locked doors and when they entered and saw me, they thought that I must be the beast that had been terrorizing them! With the Warden and his guards close on my tail, I fled out of the village and into the forest.

CHAPTER ELEVEN

'And?' prompted Lana, completely wrapped up in the story. 'What happened next?'

'After three terrifying nights, during which I barely managed to stay one step ahead of the Warden and his cronies, I found this cave. And I've been living here ever since.'

'That's terrible!' exclaimed Lana. The bear

shrugged, jolted out of his reverie.

'Every night I scour the hillsides, searching for the palace she held me in, determined to put a stop to her evil. But to no avail.'

'You never found it?'

The bear shook his head. 'I've looked everywhere, for miles around. The Hollow Tree you speak of, for example, is in what I call the Hidden Valley, just over the ridge. But however hard I search, I've not found so much as a shepherd's hut, let alone a golden palace. I understand her pain, believe me. To destroy someone's home is an act of great evil. But she has allowed her hurt to become self-pity, feeding it with acts of revenge. I have been searching for a way to end this for all of us. And finally I had an idea.'

'The potions?' guessed Lana, looking around her at the bright glass bottles.

'My grandmother was one of the cunning folk,' continued the bear. 'And a great asset to my family. I have been reminding myself of the magic I learned at her knee as a boy. This purple potion will turn me back into a man. Then, once I've explained myself to the villagers, the red potion is going to protect me from the Spider Queen's poison and the green potion will give me the strength to break my bonds and defeat her.'

'I don't understand,' said Lana.

'She will kidnap me from the Great Hall once again. Once I'm at her palace, I'll break free of the web, capture the Spider Queen and set my brother and his people free!'

'And Harrison too?' asked Lana.

'And Harrison too,' replied the bear.

'Then what are we waiting for?' asked Lana. 'Drink that purple stuff and let's hit the village.'

'There's a problem,' the bear said awkwardly.

'What?'

'It doesn't work.'

'What doesn't work?'

'The purple potion. Yet. The red one works fine. I can take any poison in the forest and remain unharmed: red cap mushrooms, deadly nightshade, you name it. And the green potion! I know I am as strong as a bear, but it's more than that. I've lifted fallen tree trunks, enlarged this cave, even crushed rocks to powder in my paws. But the purple potion . . .' The bear's voice trailed away.

'What's wrong with it?' Lana prompted.

'I can turn into any animal I want, except a man. I just have to imagine the creature I want to be: a deer, a badger, even a sparrowhawk. That's how I met the family of kites that live above me.

But however hard I try, I can't regain my human form. I fear only the Spider Queen has that power, and until she releases me from my spell, I'm stuck. That's if the Warden and his guards don't catch me first.'

'Then how am I going to find Harrison?' asked Lana.

The bear shrugged. 'Like I said, the story doesn't have a great ending.'

The two of them sat in silence for a long time, then Lana had a thought. 'What if I took your place?'

The bear raised his head.

'Give me the potions. I'll knock on the villagers' doors and tell them I'm lost and I'm looking for my brother. I'll take the potion, the one that protects you from her poison, and lie in the Great Hall, pretending to be asleep. When the Spider Queen kidnaps me, she'll lead me straight to Harrison.'

'This is a great risk for a small person such as you,' said the bear gravely. 'Fail, and you will become the next victim of the Spider Queen.'

'I've never been so sure of anything in my life,' insisted Lana. 'It's my fault Harrison's been kidnapped, and it's up to me to save him.'

The bear bowed his enormous head, his bright eyes searching the darkness, deep in thought. Then he rose to his feet, snatched a torch from the wall and examined a nearby shelf. Selecting three small bottles and replacing them in turn, he lumbered towards Lana, holding out his paw. In it were three berries: purple, green and red.

'The potions?' asked Lana.

'In berry form, so no one suspects. Put them in your pocket,' urged the bear. 'If we're doing this, it has to be now, while the hunters are off in the forest.'

The bear reached out with an enormous leathery paw, closed Lana's hand carefully around the berries, and guided it to the chest pocket of her pyjamas.

'Thanks,' said Lana. 'But I won't need the purple one, I'm already human.'

'Keep it,' replied the bear, stubbing out the torches in the sand, so that the two of them were plunged into darkness. 'You never know; it may come in handy.'

Moments later they were blinking in the moonlight. Once again, King Yashar raised himself to his full height, sampling the air cautiously.

A shadow passed over them and the bear craned his neck, scouring the treetops. 'The kite,' he whispered. 'Come.'

He parted the gorse bushes as before, then padded softly across the forest floor, with Lana running alongside him. Satisfied that he was far enough away from the kite's nest, he swung Lana up onto his shoulders and scaled the vertical trunk of an enormous spruce tree as easily as if it was lying flat on the ground.

Soon they were leaping from treetop to treetop, the lake drawing nearer with every glimpse. For the briefest of moments, clinging safely to the bear's red neckerchief, the wind rushing through her hair, Lana felt truly free. Reaching the edge of the village, they paused, swaying in the branches beside a high stockade wall.

'Where is everyone?' whispered Lana. The storm-battered huts and walkways beyond the wall appeared to be deserted, and empty boats bobbed on the water.

'Hiding. In fear of their lives,' replied the bear.

King Yashar launched himself down the tree trunk, landing silently by the door of the stockade.

'Thank you,' whispered Lana, clambering down from his back.

'One last thing,' said the bear. 'Gudrun will never let a young girl like you sleep in the Great Hall. Not while she thinks I'm on the loose. So you must keep your mission a secret.'

Lana nodded.

'Good luck,' grunted the bear, knocking on the door of the stockade.

'Wait,' said Lana. 'What happens if they turn me away?'

There was no reply. Lana looked around for the bear, but he had vanished.

A small hatch opened in the door and an indignant voice rang out. 'It's the middle of the night! Who are you and what do you want?'

CHAPTER TWELVE

'My name is Lana and I'm looking for my brother!'

A wary eye studied her though the tiny portal. 'Lana from where?'

'A long way away.'

There was a pause as the person on the other side of the door considered her answer.

'Are you armed?'

Lana shook her head and held up her hands to

show that they were empty.

There was the sound of a bolt sliding back, and the gate opened just wide enough for the owner of the wary eye to pop their head out. It belonged to a young boy, roughly her own age, with a bright, searching expression and a neat Afro. He beckoned a surprised Lana quickly inside, bolting the door behind her.

'My name's Kyle,' said the boy, puffing out his chest.

'Kyle!' exclaimed Lana. 'Gudrun's son!'

'You know my mother?' asked Kyle, suspicious.

'No,' said Lana quickly. *When was she going to learn that no one here knew anything about home?* 'How could I? I've never been here before.'

Kyle narrowed his eyes, unsure as to whether he should believe her. 'How old are you?' he asked.

'Nine.'

'I'm nine and a quarter,' said Kyle delightedly. 'And I'm taller than you. Follow me.'

'Have you done anything bad?' asked Kyle, as he led her along a wooden walkway. Lana shook her head.

'Good,' said Kyle. 'Because if you had, the Warden would put you in here.'

He pointed to a wooden contraption by the side of the path. It had three holes in it: one large and two small.

'It's called the stocks,' said Kyle gleefully. 'Your head goes in the big hole and your hands go either side. Then we all throw rotten fruit at you.'

'Thanks,' snapped Lana. 'You really know how to make someone feel welcome.' If Kyle was trying to unnerve her, it was working. 'Where are we going?'

'To see the elders,' said Kyle flatly. 'They're having a meeting.'

The path wove through a jumble of storm-damaged huts to a broken boardwalk that ran alongside the lake. Battered wooden boats nudged a short jetty, their sails stowed. One had been reduced almost to splinters. Lana noticed row after row of round objects, bobbing out in the waters of the bay.

'Oh wow,' she said. 'Balloons.'

'Those aren't balloons.' Kyle snorted. 'They're floats. To keep the nets in place.'

'Sure,' replied Lana confidently. 'Fishing nets.'

'Oyster nets,' corrected Kyle.

Those must the nets the Spider Queen was angry about, thought Lana.

They walked on in silence, past a deserted cabin with no roof.

'Why is everything so wrecked?' asked Lana.

'The storms,' replied Kyle, glancing upwards at

the restless sky. 'They're getting worse and worse. Soon there won't be anything of the village left.'

A large structure loomed on their right. It looked like a giant upturned ship. Could that be the Great Hall?

'Is that where we're going?' asked Lana casually. 'That big building there?'

Kyle shook his head without looking up.

'Good place for a meeting, I would have thought?' nudged Lana.

'Not at night,' grunted Kyle. 'In the day, maybe.'

'Why not?'

'Trust me,' he muttered darkly, 'you don't want to know.' There was a pause, during which the only sound was their footsteps on the boardwalk.

'You seem pretty young to be guarding the village?' Lana offered.

Kyle shot her a sideways glance. 'We've had

some problems,' he said, matter-of-factly. 'That's what the meeting is about. To be honest, it's what all the meetings are about.'

He left the boardwalk, trudging through the sand towards a group of huts, and Lana had to run to keep up.

'What kind of problems?' prompted Lana, keen to know if King Yashar had been telling the truth.

Kyle paused at the door of the biggest and grandest-looking hut.

'If I told you, you'd be so scared you'd go running off into the forest.'

He rapped out a rhythmic knock, and Gudrun the mayor opened the door. Or rather, someone who looked very like her.

'This is Lana,' said Kyle. 'She's looking for her brother.'

Lana couldn't help smiling but Gudrun, of course, didn't recognize her.

'Why?' asked Gudrun with concern, sweeping her long braids back over her shoulder. 'What happened to him?'

'I lost him,' said Lana, fingers crossed behind her back. 'In the forest.'

'Lost him?' Worry flashed in Gudrun's eyes. 'My dear girl, these are dangerous parts. No one is safe here, that's why we built this stockade. And even that can't keep the wretched creature out.'

'What creature?' asked Lana carefully.

'We are being terrorized,' said Gudrun. 'By a beast.'

'You again,' sneered a familiar voice. The Warden, flanked by his three guards, was marching towards them.

'You know this girl?' asked Gudrun.

'I'm the reason she's still here,' boasted the Warden. 'If it wasn't for me, she'd have been snaffled by that evil creature. We were this close, Gudrun,' he said, pinching his finger and thumb together. 'That bear won't be so lucky next time, I promise you.'

Gudrun raised her eyebrows at the Warden and turned to look at Lana. 'Darling child, I am sorry to tell you your brother isn't here. Stay the night and we'll help you look for him in the morning. Kyle here will show you to one of the empty huts.'

'Can I not stay in the Great Hall over there? It looks like there's lots of space,' asked Lana innocently.

Gudrun's face darkened. 'Absolutely not,' she declared. 'Everyone who sleeps in there gets taken by the Beast.'

Lana was burning to tell them the truth: that the bear wasn't their enemy, he was the man Gudrun had begged to come and help them. But she bit her tongue, remembering King Yashar's advice. If she wanted to find Harrison she had to keep her mission a secret.

Moments later, Kyle threw open the door to another one of the huts. Inside was a hearth with a crackling fire, a table and a comfy-looking bed. On the table was a loaf of crusty bread and a glistening hunk of rich-looking cheese. Next to it, a flagon held cool, crystal-clear water. Suddenly realizing how hungry she was, Lana fell on the food, devouring it quickly. The simple meal was one of the most delicious things she'd ever tasted.

'Feeling better?' asked Kyle, smiling at Lana.

She nodded, kicking off her boots so that she

could warm her frozen toes by the fire. Now that she was inside, she realized how cold she had been in just her pyjamas and empty wellies. Noticing her wrap her arms around herself, Kyle picked up a warm-looking tunic and a pair of knee-length socks and passed them over to her.

'Here, take these,' he said kindly. 'They might be a bit big, but they're warm and dry.'

'Thank you,' Lana said, snuggling into the cosy tunic.

'What do you think of my mum, then?' Kyle asked suddenly.

'She seems really nice,' replied Lana. 'Maybe a bit stressed?'

Kyle nodded, considering her answer. 'She's a princess,' he said proudly. 'And my dad is a prince. His name is Zephir. But he was taken by the Beast.'

There was a pause and Kyle looked down at his shoes, determined not to catch her eye. Lana wanted badly to say that King Yashar had already told her, but again she managed to keep it to herself. The whole plan rested on sticking to her story.

'Don't worry,' she said gently. 'I'm sure he'll be okay.'

'I'm not scared,' said Kyle, looking up suddenly with pain in his eyes. 'If that's what you're thinking. If that bear comes anywhere near this village, I'll finish him with this.' He held up a spear solemnly, then turned to leave the room. 'Get some sleep. I'll see you in the morning.'

Lana waited patiently, listening to his retreating footsteps. Then, as soon as he was gone, she slipped out of the door and along the boardwalk, to where the Great Hall loomed in the moonlight.

She tried the two enormous doors at the front, but they were locked. Like a shadow, she flitted around the building, searching for a way in. As she turned the far corner, two bright eyes and a row of white fangs sprang out suddenly from the darkness!

KSSSSSSS!!!!

Lana yelped in alarm!

It was a cat. She sighed with relief.

'*Sssh*, little one,' she whispered. 'Don't be scared. It's only me, Lana.'

The cat angled its head, uncertain. Lana crouched down and reached out her hand, rubbing her finger and thumb together to make the kind of noise cats find impossible to resist.

Curious, the cat padded closer.

'Where did you come from?' soothed Lana, stroking the back of its head. Its fur was deep grey and as soft as down. The cat looked up at her meaningfully.

Then it sprang away into the darkness and disappeared.

Lana frowned, baffled as to where it had gone. Stooping down and peering after it, she saw that there was a gap under the wall. The cat had shown her how to get into the Great Hall!

After a quick glance to make sure no one was watching, Lana rolled over onto her back, shut her eyes and wriggled inside.

When she opened them again, the first thing she saw was the full moon, framed by shifting cloud, beaming in through a large square hole in the roof. The second thing was the grey cat, standing on the pale floor, lit by a crisp rectangle of moonlight.

She pushed herself to her feet, breathing in the

musty air. There were cobwebs everywhere.

The cat miaowed and sprang up onto a long bench, lined with animal skins. Moving closer, Lana saw that the bench was one of a pair, standing either side of a large fireplace, piled high with grey ash.

This must be where they sleep, she thought.

The cat trotted closer, pressing its back against her hand, inviting her to stroke it. Lana obliged gratefully, happy to have a friend in this cold, deserted place.

Which was when the cat leaped down from the bench, scampered across the floor and vanished back through the gap under the wall.

Lana felt her heart sink as the reality of her mission took shape in her mind.

Am I up to this? she asked herself breathlessly, sitting down on the bench.

No matter how frightened she felt now, it might be so much worse for Harrison. What if he was wrapped in golden thread, in the Spider Queen's larder, alongside the warriors from the village? Somehow, she had to find the courage to see this through.

Fishing in her pyjama pocket, she found the three berries, selecting the red one to protect her from the Spider Queen's poison. She squished it between her teeth, its sour flavour sending shudders down her arms and back.

She settled down on the bench, pulling animal skins over her.

Then she lay, staring at the ceiling, waiting for the Spider Queen.

CHAPTER THIRTEEN

Lana wasn't sure how long she stayed in the darkness of the Great Hall, listening to the wind and watching dark clouds shutter the rounded moon. It might have been three minutes or three hours. She was just beginning to wonder whether the Spider Queen would ever come, when something moved on the floor, catching her eye. Silhouetted in the rectangular patch of moonlight was an enormous spider,

dangling from a thick thread, legs twitching!

Lana caught her breath, panic surging through her. Her eyes darted up to the skylight. At the end of a golden thread dangled a tiny spider, no bigger than a coin. The huge shape on the floor was just a shadow! As the spider descended towards her, she took several deep breaths and lay back down. *This must be the Spider Queen*, she reasoned, *come to capture me. I can't let her know I'm awake.*

An anxious thought brought her lurching back up to a sitting position. She had forgotten to eat the green berry, the one that gave you strength! Without it she might never be able to break free of the Spider Queen's cocoon.

Glancing upwards, she saw that the tiny spider was halfway down from the roof, moving rapidly on its silken thread. Scrabbling in her pyjama pocket, she fished out the berry. But she was so eager to get it to her lips that she fumbled, and it fell to the floor, disappearing between two floorboards.

Rolling off the bench, she tried to hook it out with the tip of her finger, only managing to push it further down into the crack!

It was no use: she would have to carry on without it. Clambering back onto the bench, she leaned her head back and closed her eyes.

With the lightest of touches, the creature landed on the back of her exposed hand. Lana swallowed anxiously, summoning every ounce of her courage. She felt the tiniest of scratches, and then a strange warm feeling flooded her entire body.

It's bitten me! she thought. She felt her body tense, as whatever medicine was in the red berry fought a valiant battle with whatever poison was in the spider's bite. Then suddenly the room began to blur around her, fading into darkness . . .

Like a bubble rising to the surface, Lana's mind burst into consciousness. It was a struggle to open her eyes, and when she finally succeeded, she found herself peering out through strands of gold. Her arms were pinned to her sides, her legs bound. She was encased in golden thread! Above her, a now-familiar figure appeared in the skylight, two golden gloves circling one another, hand over hand, as if hauling in an invisible rope.

'The Spider Queen!' breathed Lana.

Something pulled at her feet, and suddenly she was dangling in the air, upside down, with the fireplace swinging beneath her. The Spider Queen was up on the roof, heaving her up!

As she reached the rafters, two strong hands grasped her ankles, dragging her up onto the windswept roof. Lana let her body go limp, determined not to let her captor know she was awake.

'Well, well, well!' she heard the Spider Queen whisper. 'If it isn't the girl! I knew I'd find you eventually. Time to join your brother.'

Lana felt herself being slung over the Spider Queen's bony shoulder. Cautiously, she opened one eye to see that she was being carried along the roof of the Great Hall! Her plan was working!

Suddenly, the Spider Queen froze.

Voices drifted up from the boardwalk and Lana held her breath, listening carefully. Below them, Gudrun and the Warden were in deep discussion.

'One moment,' said Gudrun. 'I want to check on the girl.'

'Yes,' said the Warden. 'I've been meaning to talk to you about her.'

'Oh?' asked Gudrun.

'This story of hers,' continued the Warden. 'I'd take it with several large pinches of salt. Maybe even a fistful.'

'And why is that?'

'I think she may be in league with the bear.'

Lana sensed the Spider Queen was listening with interest.

'We nearly caught him tonight, up in the forest, but he vanished into thin air. In his place was the girl. When we questioned her, she threw us off the scent.'

There was a pause, then Gudrun said in a clear voice, 'Or maybe you're just looking for someone to blame? She's a young girl in a dangerous place, looking for her lost brother, and she deserves our help.'

There was a pause. The Spider Queen shifted Lana off her shoulder, and onto the rushes that covered the roof, so that they were face to face. Forgetting she was meant to be asleep, Lana opened her eyes.

The Spider Queen recoiled in alarm.

'What is this?' she hissed, dropping Lana's wrist as if it was red hot.

'Help!' yelled Lana, shouting above the wind.

'Halt!' called the Warden from down below. 'Who goes there?'

But the Spider Queen ignored him, hidden from view by the angle of the roof. 'You're awake!' she barked at Lana. 'How can this be? I bit you, didn't I?'

Snatching Lana's hand towards her, she examined the bite. Seeing the red mark on Lana's skin, her confusion curdled to anger.

'Trick me with magic, would you? Well, I have a few tricks of my own!'

Touching the gold necklace around her neck, the Spider Queen arced a long bony arm in the air, and a wild wind whipped up, unleashing a tornado of dust and leaves, while high above, dark clouds blotted out the moon.

Down on the ground, the Warden blew his hunting horn. 'Guards!' he called. 'Come quick!'

The Spider Queen slid off her glove, holding up a long sharp golden thumbnail as if it were a tiny dagger.

Helpless, Lana gulped, fearing the worst. But instead of harming her, the Spider Queen used her nail to slit the cocoon from top to bottom before whipping it off like a magician pulling away a tablecloth.

Then once again, she touched the gold necklace, throwing her free hand into the air, and a bolt of lightning raced down from the sky, striking a tall tree just beyond the stockade! Its upper branches caught fire, burning furiously.

Down on the ground, Gudrun and the Warden immediately ran for cover.

As lights appeared in the nearby huts, the Spider Queen angled the empty cocoon into the wind, so that it billowed with air. She was about to take off!

'Wait!' demanded Lana, clutching at the Spider Queen's cape. 'Where's my brother?'

'You want to save him,' said the Spider Queen, in mock sympathy, as a clap of thunder bellowed overhead. 'Don't worry, I'll let him know you tried. This will not be the last time we meet, girl.'

Then the cocoon caught the wind and raced up into the night sky, taking the Spider Queen with it.

CHAPTER FOURTEEN

For several minutes Lana lay on the roof of the Great Hall, trying to process what had happened. The skies opened and it began to pour with rain. Then the shock of the near-escape took hold of her, and her shoulders began to shake as she dragged air into her lungs with racking sobs.

The Spider Queen had vanished! How was she going to find Harrison now?

Raising her head, she saw a ladder appear beside her and moments later one of the Warden's guards was carrying her to safety. As they reached the boardwalk, raindrops bouncing like glass beads, Kyle came running up, clutching his spear.

'Where is it?' he snarled, through gritted teeth. 'Where's the Beast?'

'Gone,' barked the Warden, taking charge. 'You three: I want a headcount, make sure everyone's safe.'

Without a word, his three sidekicks ran off to do his bidding.

Lana felt a gentle hand on her shoulder. Gudrun was at her side, helping her to her feet, guiding her under the overhang to shield her from the rain. 'Are you all right?' she asked with concern, brushing away Lana's tears. 'It didn't hurt you, did it?'

Still sobbing, Lana shook her head.

'My poor girl,' soothed Gudrun. 'Stolen from your hut, after you came to us for help and protection. What a terrible fright! Come, you can sleep with me and Kyle.'

Kyle was eyeing Lana suspiciously, and Lana felt a pang of guilt. Should she come clean and tell Gudrun about her mission?

'It must have dragged her up there,' Gudrun continued to the Warden, nodding up at the roof of the Great Hall. 'So that it couldn't be seen. I shudder to think what it would have done next.'

'No,' said Lana, suddenly finding her voice. 'That's not what happened.'

The rain on the boardwalk seemed to beat even more loudly as several villagers turned towards her with interest. Lana fixed her eyes on Gudrun and continued. 'I went to sleep in the Great Hall.'

There was an audible gasp.

'But . . . why?' Gudrun asked, mystified. 'We expressly told you not to go in there – it is far too dangerous.'

'To try and catch the Spider Queen.'

Gudrun and the Warden shared a confused look. 'Sorry,' said the Warden. 'Who?'

'The Spider Queen. She's the one behind all this.

If we can find out where she lives, then maybe we can stop her.'

'The. Spider. Queen,' repeated the Warden carefully, emphasizing each word in turn. 'And she would be what? A woman?'

'Yes,' said Lana. 'Well, more like a witch.'

'A witch.' The Warden nodded, removing his skull cap and shaking it free of water. 'In that case, what's that big furry thing me and my guards have been chasing?'

'King Yashar!' blurted Lana. 'Disguised as a bear!'

'King Yashar?' echoed Gudrun. 'He was taken by the Beast.'

The Warden turned to Gudrun, eyebrows raised.

'It's true!' exclaimed Lana. 'The Spider Queen kidnapped him, then when he wouldn't do as she said, she turned him into a bear so he'd get the blame.'

'There's no Spider Queen living anywhere near here, Lana,' said Gudrun gently.

'There is, I promise. In a giant golden palace.'

There was a long pause while everyone avoided everyone else's eye. Everyone, that was, except Kyle, who just stared at Lana.

'I'm calling a village council,' said Gudrun, making it clear that the subject was closed for now. 'Kyle, you can sleep with me tonight and we'll give Lana your room. The poor girl is so shaken, she's dreaming.'

'Whatever,' said Kyle.

'Goodnight, Lana,' said Gudrun firmly. 'Try and get some rest.'

Which was how Lana found herself alone, lying on Kyle's bed, trying to figure out a new plan. One that would finally lead her to the palace of the Spider Queen. But rack her brains as she might, no ideas came. Drumming rain lashed the creaking walls of the hut, the wind howling sorrowfully as she tossed and turned. In her mind's eye, she glimpsed Harrison, alone in the Spider Queen's larder, cocooned in golden thread. Then King Yashar in his cave, waiting anxiously for her return. Finally, as she drifted into sleep, she saw the Hollow Tree, its long branches bending in the wind, calling to her.

Lana opened her eyes as a string of thunderclaps morphed into the sound of someone knocking at her door. The shutters had blown open in the night, and a grey dawn was peeking through banks of blustery cloud.

Kyle burst in, out of breath. 'You're wanted.'

He gulped. 'At the meeting.'

He handed her a leather bag with a bone stopper in the top of it. 'What's this?' asked Lana.

'Breakfast,' replied Kyle. 'It's nearly dawn. You can drink as we walk.'

Outside, the wind was blowing stronger than ever, and the tall trees surrounding the stockade were swaying restlessly.

As they stepped along the boardwalk, Lana loosened the stopper and sniffed the contents of the bag.

'Smells funny,' she said. 'What is it?'

'Goat's milk,' Kyle replied.

Lana's empty stomach got the better of her and she began to drink. The milk was warm and sweet, with a sour edge. Lana, whose favourite food was pickles, decided she was never having anything else on her cornflakes ever again.

'That bear's lucky,' said Kyle. 'If he'd come for me, I'd have jabbed him with my spear. See the end of it there? It's real metal.'

Lana nodded, wiping her lip as they stopped outside the doors to the Great Hall.

The meeting was in full swing, and Gudrun was speaking.

'Lana, welcome,' she said as they entered. 'We've lost too many brave souls to this dreadful Beast, as everyone here knows. But last night he stooped lower than ever: he tried to kidnap this poor child. Our attempts to capture him have failed.' Gudrun turned to look pointedly at the Warden. 'Meanwhile our village is being wrecked by storms and our Great Hall is only safe to enter during the day. We need to put our heads together. Does anyone have any information they might share? No detail is too small.'

An elderly woman put her hand up. 'Oysters,' she said.

'Oysters?' asked Gudrun. 'Can you expand on that at all?'

'He's stealing them,' said the woman. There was a murmuring and muttering in the crowd. 'They keep disappearing from the barrel.'

Lana froze as she remembered the midnight snack the bear had served her. So that was where he got them from!

'Good,' said Gudrun. 'That's something to work with. Any ideas?'

The Warden shrugged.

'Leave him some salt and pepper?' he joked. His three guards laughed, but no one else did.

'How about we set a trap?'

Everyone turned towards Kyle.

'We could set one of these in the oyster tank.'

He held up a vicious-looking metal contraption, with jagged iron teeth. 'When the bear comes prowling, he'll get a handshake he'll never forget!'

A murmur of approval chased around the hut.

'Not bad,' agreed the Warden. 'Not bad at all. And when we catch him, where will we put him?'

'In the stocks!' announced Kyle, and a loud cheer went up. Gudrun smiled proudly.

Lana shrank back in horror, her mind racing. Somehow, she had to warn King Yashar, before it was too late.

CHAPTER FIFTEEN

No sooner had Lana decided to warn the bear about the trap than the door was flung open behind her and a group of anxious villagers burst into the Great Hall.

'The stockade!' bellowed the first.

'It's down!' shouted the second.

'What they said,' wheezed the third, who was slightly less fit.

'Meeting adjourned!' called Gudrun, as everyone rushed to the door.

Outside, the Spider Queen's storm was raging harder than ever and a wild wind had brought down the lightning-struck spruce. It had crashed through the stockade wall, flattening a broad section. The sky was dark with thunderclouds, there were high waves on the lake and the already-wet sand was spotting with fresh rain.

'Quick!' called Gudrun, struggling to make herself heard in the gale. 'We have to fix it.'

But as everyone rushed forward to help, Lana held back. Could this be her chance to warn King Yashar?

She glanced in the direction of the gate. A fearsome-looking woman was guarding it, and Lana didn't fancy her chances of getting past her.

The lake? Perhaps she could escape that way.

Casting her eyes to the jetty, she spied a clutch of boats dancing on the water. Might she steal one? No. Useless. The waves were too high, the wind too strong.

Frustrated, she turned back towards the crowd. A downpour began, the Warden shouting instructions as his guards struggled to lift a fallen fence pole in the driving rain. As they battled, more villagers swarmed around them, raising their hands to help. Lana frowned. They were all so focused on their task. Could she somehow slip past them and escape through the gap in the stockade?

She was edging forward, calculating her chances, when a distant movement caught her eye. The woman guarding the gate had abandoned her post and – sheltering under a wool shawl – was running to lend a hand!

It was now or never.

Lana backed up slowly, until she was out of sight, then raced through the huts, fighting against the wind, heading for the gate.

Closing the heavy door carefully behind her, Lana ran up through the forest, making for the line of rocks at the lip of the valley. As the ground got steeper, she glanced back at the village, just visible beyond the farthest trees. The stockade wall was nearly back in place! She needed to find the bear, before anyone noticed she was missing.

But as she neared the ridge, it dawned on Lana that King Yashar's cave would be almost impossible to find. The pale morning sun was buried in cloud, making everything dark and gloomy, and every patch of forest looked the same. Everywhere she looked, she saw gorse bushes, each identical to the one that surrounded her new friend's home. She might be right next to the cave and never know!

To make matters worse, the rain turned to hail. Terrifying fist-sized lumps of ice came rattling down through the trees like cannonballs, crashing onto the forest floor in a flurry of pine needles.

Nowhere in the forest was safe, and Lana was forced to shelter under an outcrop of rock. Shivering and scared, she hugged her knees, willing her luck to change. *I just need to find the bear*, she told herself. *He'll know what to do. Maybe together, we can explain to Gudrun about the Spider Queen's spell. And he can conjure up some magic to help us find the Golden Palace, and rescue Harrison and the kidnapped villagers.*

As the clouds broke and the hail stopped suddenly, she emerged from her hiding place to see a shadow flitting over her. She flinched, thinking

she was about to be struck by the biggest hailstone ever. But as her eyes chased the shadow across the rocks, it suddenly came into focus as the sharp outline of a bird.

Of course! The kite!

There he was now, circling above the trees.

As she watched, he plummeted to the ground, disappearing from view. To Lana, that meant only one thing: he had caught something. And that something was about to provide breakfast for his hungry partner . . .

Moments later the bird rose into view, clutching a mouse in his talons. He made a wide circuit of the treetops to get his bearings, then headed off across the forest.

Lana immediately took off after him, dodging through the trees, doing her best to keep him in sight. For several long breathless minutes they journeyed together, girl and bird, until once again the kite began to circle.

'Come on, Mr Kite,' whispered Lana to herself. 'Show me your nest.'

As though he could hear her, the bird began to beat his wings rapidly, landing in the upper branches of a tall spruce. Lana glimpsed a large nest, with what appeared to be a mother and her eggs.

Moments later, Lana was unpicking the gorse bushes, just as she had seen King Yashar do. The thorns were even longer and sharper than she remembered, and she managed to give herself a nasty jab, right between her thumb and finger, that made her want to howl with pain. But she remembered the bear's warning, that the nest above her mustn't be disturbed, and held her tongue.

Hopefully her clever friend would have a potion to put on it, once she was inside. 'King Yashar!' she hissed, peering into the darkness. 'Are you in there?'

She tried to crawl forward, but something caught her foot. It was probably a root, she decided, trying to shake herself free. But it wouldn't let go.

Huffing with annoyance, she backed out of the entrance and turned to see what it was.

It was a man's hand.

And it belonged to the Warden.

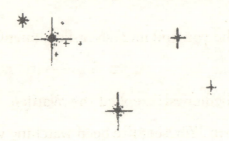

CHAPTER SIXTEEN

'Hold still,' said the Warden, tying Lana's wrists. Distant thunder rolled across the sky and rain continued to fall.

'Ow!' gasped Lana. 'That hurts!'

'It's meant to,' said the Warden, grinning.

One of his three guards was slashing away at the gorse, while the other two held back a pack of snarling hounds. Lana glanced anxiously at the entrance to the cave, praying that Yashar wasn't inside.

'How did you find me?' she asked, burning with fury.

'Can I be honest?' replied the Warden. 'A little bit too easily. You see, I've been watching you very carefully. I saw the look on your face when Kyle came up with the idea of the trap, and I thought to myself: *that's the look of a traitor*. Then, when I realized you'd slipped away . . .'

Lana scowled. 'You followed me!'

'I'm afraid so.' The Warden nodded. 'Because unlike your beastly friend,' he nodded again, this time at the bear's cave, 'you forgot to hide your scent.'

Lana felt herself flush with shame.

'You poor girl,' said the Warden, smiling to himself. 'That bear must be your only friend in this strange place, and you feel bad because you led us right to him. Don't worry, you'll soon be

'Spare me the song and dance, please,' said the Warden

spending *lots* of time together. In the stocks!'

'But we're innocent!' protested Lana. 'I keep telling you!'

The Warden narrowed his eyes.

'Spare me the song and dance, please. You were hiding him, weren't you? When I first met you?'

Lana shook her head, but her eyes gave her away. 'No! I mean, yes, but—'

'That's why you came to the village, isn't it? To spy on us!'

'I've told you why I came!' protested Lana. 'To catch the Spider Queen!'

But the Warden wasn't listening. Instead, he put his hunting horn to his lips, and blew a series of short sharp notes.

The hounds began to bark, straining at their leashes.

'Tally-ho!' he bellowed, and the entire pack

149

came racing up the bank. They poured into the cave entrance, baying furiously.

'Stop!' yelled Lana. 'Stop!'

The Warden began a hearty chuckle, but the smile froze on his face as a terrifying growl sounded from inside the cave. It was followed by a high yelp, as if one of the dogs had been hurt.

The Warden glanced anxiously behind him. 'Stand by!' he called, and all three guards primed their bows.

From the cave came more growls, and more hysterical barking and yelping. Suddenly, out charged the bear, wheeling round and round, swiping with his front paws as the dogs nipped and snapped at him from every angle!

'Fire!' called the Warden, and the guards released a volley of arrows.

But the bear was too fast for them, batting their

shots aside as easily as if they were flies.

'Run, Yashar, run!' hollered Lana.

The bear locked eyes with Lana, confusion flashing across his face.

'It wasn't my fault!' called Lana. 'They tricked me!'

But the damage was done. Sadness filled the bear's eyes, and his shoulders dropped, defeated. The hounds, sensing that the fight had left him, circled closer, baying excitedly.

The Warden pulled back an arrow, grinned, then let it fly. It struck deep into the bear's shoulder.

King Yashar stared at the wound for a few seconds, then plucked the arrow out. His eyes seemed glassy, as if he was having difficulty focusing. He swayed slightly, teetered, then collapsed heavily to the ground.

'Poison arrows,' explained the Warden,

triumphantly. 'I keep a little bottle of tincture here, in this clever waist bag I invented. Back, back!' he called. He gave a short blast on the horn, and the hounds reluctantly retreated. The last of them was unable to resist nipping at the bear's flank.

'Oi!' he yelled at the dog, chasing him away from the enormous prone body of the bear.

'Quick, we'd better record this – the moment I bested the Beast! It'll make a good tapestry.' The Warden grinned, placing his foot on the bear's head. One of the guards produced a piece of framed cloth and began to sew furiously.

'Get your foot off his head!' bellowed Lana. 'That's cruel!'

'It's justice, snowflake,' said the Warden. 'You know what they say. If you can't do the time, don't do the crime. And you two are going to do a *lot* of time.'

'Three days and nights.' The female guard grinned. 'While we throw rotten fruit at you.'

'Not just rotten fruit,' added another, still working away with his needle. 'We throw all sorts. Dog sick. Chicken poo. The brown water in the bottom of the lavatory-brush holder. There,' he announced, holding up his work for his master's inspection. 'How about that?'

The Warden examined the needlework. 'Hmm . . .' he mused. 'Can you make my muscles bigger?'

'But we're innocent!' protested Lana, interrupting the Warden's preening. 'I told you! He tried to save the village!'

The Warden smiled to himself and shook his head.

'You can drop the story now,' he said. 'In case you hadn't realized, this is over.'

No sooner had he spoken than the bear reared up from the ground, eyes wide. He pinned the Warden to the trunk of a nearby tree with one giant paw.

'Eeaargghhh!' screamed the Warden.

'Run, Lana, run!' bellowed King Yashar.

'Don't just stand there!' wailed the Warden, quaking in terror. 'Shoot!'

'Right away, Sire!' One of the henchmen fumbled with his bow.

'Now!' bellowed King Yashar.

'I'm so sorry!' Lana yelled.

'Before it's too late!'

Lana didn't wait to see what happened next. She did as her friend had told her, and ran.

CHAPTER SEVENTEEN

It wasn't long before Lana heard the dogs behind her. The bear had bought her some time, but by the sound of their barking, it wasn't much.

How could I have been so stupid? she scolded herself as she raced through the forest. *I led them right to him!*

Her legs felt weak with exhaustion and she paused, listening for the dogs. Their barking was getting louder! She stumbled forward, crashing over wet bracken. Then, just when she felt she could go no further, she heard the sound she had been listening for: the chattering stream that marked the crossing point to the Hidden Valley.

Gasping for breath, she staggered through the last of the trees to find she was in the spot where she had first met the bear.

There was no time to waste. She plunged into the water, hoping it would disguise her scent, and splashed round the bend in the stream before scrambling up through the babbling waters to where the maze of giant boulders guarded the entrance to the Hidden Valley.

Reaching the top, she chanced a look back. Through the trees below, she glimpsed the guards' horses rearing in the water as the hounds wheeled around them, unsure which direction to take.

Lana gulped air into her lungs. It was now daylight, and dark clouds had gathered over the lake. There was a strange slanting haze beneath them that must be torrential rain.

Poor Gudrun. The Spider Queen had wrecked the village with lightning, and now she was trying to wash away the huts!

'Goodbye, Gudrun,' Lana said to herself. 'I'm sorry I couldn't help you.'

The hounds brought her back to reality. They had picked up her scent and were now tearing along the stream, closely followed by the three guards. She could guess what had happened: the Warden was taking the bear to the village alone, so he could get all the credit, leaving his flunkies to track her down. She had to get out of here, fast.

Squeezing through a gap in the rock, she followed the stream up through the maze of giant boulders towards the ridge. Reaching the pool at the top of the waterfall, she picked up the animal track, which led her up around the large flat rock and over into the strange hush of the snow-drenched Hidden Valley.

Cold air sliced her like a knife, and she pulled the sleeves of the tunic that Kyle had given her over her hands as she crashed down through the trees in giant strides.

The hounds! She could hear shouting, back on the other side of the ridge. Her pursuers hadn't yet found a way through. She breathed a sigh of relief which quickly became a gasp of horror, when the first dog emerged from beside the large flat rock and began to chase down the hillside towards her!

A surge of adrenaline threw Lana forward, like a wave catching hold of a surfboard. Suddenly she was sprinting out of the forest, across the clearing, heading for the Hollow Tree!

Her heart raced as she shook the snow from the lowest-hanging branch, swung her leg over it, then shimmied up. Or at least, she tried to . . . Her hands were still tied, and there were so many fiddly branches in her way!

Gritting her teeth, she continued hauling herself upwards. The lead dog skidded to a halt in the snow beneath her and Lana squirmed higher, glancing down just in time to see its jaws snap shut right where her pink wellington boot had just been.

Blood thumping in her ears, Lana pushed herself up into a standing position, climbing higher while the dogs circled beneath her, leaping and barking.

But she still wasn't safe. There was a shout from

up on the ridge. She held up her hand, shielding her eyes from the morning sun. The three guards were riding down through the snow.

With one final effort, she swung herself up into the crown of the tree. Finally, there it was: the hollow that would lead her to safety.

She peered down into the darkness, and was astonished to see two men and a woman wearing yellow hard hats peering up towards her! Their voices boomed out of the top of the tree, amplified by the hollow.

'IS ANYONE IN THERE?'

Lana pulled herself back before she was seen.

'THIS TREE IS ABOUT TO BE FELLED! YOU HAVE TEN MINUTES TO VACATE THE AREA!'

Lana held her breath.

What was going on? Carl had promised her that

he would protect the tree! Once it was felled, there would be no way back. Harrison would be left in this strange world for ever, a prisoner of the Spider Queen. And she would be stuck in everyday life, without her brother.

In a daze, she stared down at the barking dogs, then back again at the hollow.

This is all my fault, she told herself. *Every last bit of it. If only I'd helped the spiders. Then the Spider Queen would never have come looking for me!*

There was a rumble of thunder from a large black cloud overhead. It began to snow, and the cold flakes mingled with her tears.

'What do I do?' she pleaded quietly. 'What do I *do*?' But the only answer was the rushing of the wind and the baying of the hounds.

She felt a tickle on her hand. Thinking that it must be a snowflake, she gave it a shake. But the tickle was still there. And it was moving. Wiping her eyes, she focused her gaze.

It was a Golden Diving Bell spider: she could tell by the distinctive pattern on its body. Smiling through her tears, she let it run over her fingers, catching it first in one hand, then the other. Where had it come from?

The hollow! It must have climbed up from the marsh!

She held it closer, wondering at how small and perfect it was. Then, as she watched, it made a wriggling movement, and to her amazement, took off on the breeze. For a moment, she could hardly believe what she had just seen. Not only did they spin golden thread and build homes underwater, it now appeared that Golden Diving Bell spiders could fly!

She frowned, feeling a pang of regret. How could

she have thought these fascinating creatures weren't worth saving? And how tragic would it be if they disappeared for ever, just because a few selfish humans couldn't be bothered to find them a new home? If only there was a way for her to help them . . .

A thought suddenly struck her.

She still had the purple berry!

Or did she? Twisting her bound hands, she awkwardly unbuttoned the tunic and fished in the pocket of her pyjamas. Where was it? Had it fallen out while she was running? Then the tip of her finger found what she was looking for: a cold, round, smooth shape, nestling in the very bottom corner of her pocket.

A purple berry, perfect as a pearl.

The purple berry turns you into any animal, King Yashar had said. *All you have to do is imagine it.*

Lana couldn't get to Harrison and she couldn't escape the dogs.

But maybe, just maybe, there was a way to save the spiders.

CHAPTER EIGHTEEN

For a few seconds, Lana crouched there in the crown of the Hollow Tree, her mind whirring, dogs barking, snow falling and the wind chasing through the tops of the fir trees like waves on a stormy ocean.

The plan that was taking shape was so crazy, so daring, as to be barely possible. But the more she tried to ignore it, the clearer it became.

She was going to turn herself into a Golden

Diving Bell spider!

Only then would she be able to warn the spiders in the marsh of the danger they were in and bring them back to safety. Then maybe – once her eight-legged friends were safe and sound – she could use her spider powers to fly over the dogs, find the Golden Palace and rescue Harrison!

She took a deep breath, picturing a Golden Diving Bell spider. Pinching the berry carefully between her finger and thumb, she popped it in her mouth and bit down hard. She felt the cold juice coat her tongue: a mixture of under-ripe cranberry and blackcurrant that was so sour it made her shudder.

She opened her eyes.

Nothing had changed. The dark cloud was still above her, fizzing with electricity, and the wind was pounding the trees of the forest.

Was it working?

She felt a strange feeling in her throat. She tried to swallow, but her mouth seemed not to work the way that it usually did. And was it her imagination, or were the ropes that tied her growing larger and looser?

Then she realized – it wasn't the world around her that was getting bigger, *she* was getting smaller!

Large black hairs were springing from her wrists! She felt a stabbing pain in her chest and looked down to see that she was sprouting new arms on both sides. Or were they legs? Everything seemed to be dividing – there were eight images swimming in front of her. She had eight eyes!

It was really happening – she was turning into a spider!

The confusion that surrounded her suddenly merged into one single super-powered spider vision, bristling with detail. Everywhere she looked there were colours she had never seen before: in the lichens and mosses of the Hollow Tree, in the fur of the dogs as they leaped below her, and in the eyes of the three guards as they stared up at her. It was as if she had spent her whole life in a blur and the world had only just come into focus.

And as the world came into focus, so did her mission. She needed to act fast.

Spinning round, she saw she was on the lip of the hollow, a vast chasm that seemed as wide as the crater of a volcano. She circled round it, pondering the best plan of attack. It was the strangest feeling, to suddenly be in the body of a creature she had always found scary. The sight of her own giant hairy legs undulating in front of her filled her with a mix of wonder and loathing.

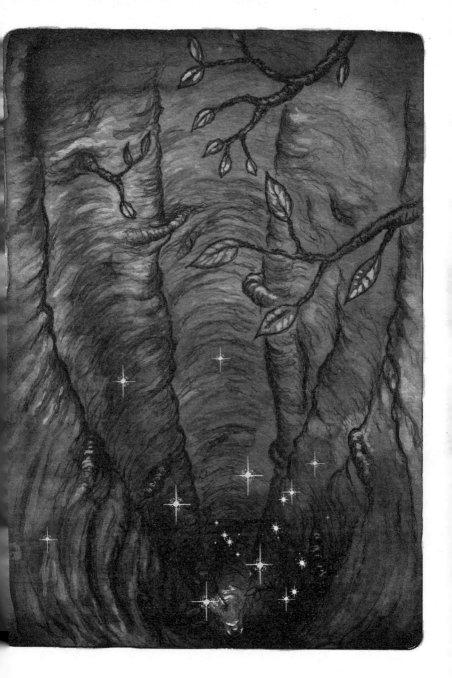

A shaft of daylight was visible way below her

Cautiously, she peered over into the void. The three workers had vanished and a shaft of daylight was visible way below her, like the pale reflection at the bottom of a very deep well. Then, as she watched, the unmistakable sound of a motorized saw boomed up through the hollow. They were about to start! She felt a twinge of despair. She was now so small compared to the tree that it would take her hours, maybe days to climb down, and by then it might be too late.

But wait.

Maybe she could use her thread!

Tensing her body, she touched it with one of her legs, drawing out a great gobbet of liquid silk that quickly hardened in the air to form a misshapen golden lump. She tried again, drawing the liquid out faster, and this time she produced a thread!

Thinking hard, she drew out more liquid silk

and attached the end to an outcrop of bark. She now had an anchor. All she needed to do, she decided, was jump. Taking a deep breath, she launched herself into the hollow.

Down, down, down she plunged, the golden thread spooling out behind her, making her almost weightless. She felt giddy with excitement and her mind flashed back to a video Harrison had once shown her of astronauts in the International Space Station, floating in mid-air with their air supply lines trailing behind them, helpless with laughter as they tried to drink jelly-like blobs of liquid or eat a chocolate bar. This was exactly how they must feel! Who knew spiders had this much fun?

Before she knew it, she was landing on a dried leaf the size of a circus tent on the mossy floor of the hollow. Gripping the tiny veins on its surface, she bobbed up and down, waiting for it to settle.

Above her loomed four giant holes the size of cathedral windows, and she smiled a spider smile to herself as she recognized them as the eyes, nose and mouth of the Hollow Tree. After scuttling rapidly along a large twig – it was like scaling a giant oil pipe – she launched herself up the inside of the trunk, so that she was looking out through the Hollow Tree's open mouth.

The early-morning sun was blinding and it took a moment for her super-powered spider eyes to adjust. The first person she saw was Carl, issuing orders. He was no longer in his Warden outfit, bellowing from the top of his horse. Here he was in a yellow hard hat and jacket, gesturing to one of his workers, who was holding a powerful chainsaw. This close up, the sound was almost deafening, bristling over every hair on her body. Lana felt a tide of anger rise up within her.

Carl had betrayed her. He really was about to cut down the tree!

Without hesitation, Lana leaped out into the light, trailing the thread behind her. Then, after making the softest of landings on a mossy tree root, she raced along a channel in its bark, onto the dark mud of the marsh. She wove her way quickly through a towering forest of grasses until she reached the edge of a vast stretch of water.

She needed to find a spider, and that meant she had to dive.

Anxiously, she glanced up. The worker with the chainsaw was right by the tree, preparing to make his first cut! She had seconds left!

Winding the thread around a convenient pebble, she launched herself forward and plunged into the water. The harsh sound of the saw vanished, and the treacly liquid felt luxurious and soft, like rolling in velvet. Spooling out more thread, she let gravity pull her slowly down. Her eight feet kicked up tiny puffs of mud as they struck the bottom.

Turning round and round on the spot, she scoured the surrounding waters. The detail was almost overwhelming: there, stuck to luminous blue-green reeds were technicoloured fish eggs the size of space hoppers, giant larvae as bright as clownfish and mother-of-pearl water snails the size of bouncy castles.

Then, far off in the distance she spotted a golden glimmer. A nest!

That must be why the spiders made their homes out of gold thread, so that they would be able to find them easily in the murky water.

Legs and belly tingling with excitement, she rushed towards it with giant strides. There must be a door somewhere? She crawled up over the outside of the dome, but there was no way in.

She felt herself becoming lightheaded and swam for the surface, gasping for air. As she watched, the workman's saw bit into the ancient bark of the Hollow Tree, its vibrations becoming even more high-pitched and urgent!

She dived back under.

Focus. She had to focus. What had Professor North told her?

The entrance to the diving-bell home was at the bottom of the nest. She needed to crawl downwards, over its gleaming, balloon-like surface.

There it was: a convenient spider-sized hole. She was now almost bursting for breath!

With a pulse of her legs, she was inside the chamber of the nest. Breathing deeply, she filled her starved lungs with delicious-tasting air.

But the nest was empty. She needed to find

another: one whose occupant was at home.

She was turning to leave when her legs were swept out from under her, sending her crashing to the floor! Fast-moving limbs rolled her over and over, coating her in sticky golden thread, then hauled her up in the air like a bauble on a Christmas tree.

A friendly-looking furry face with eight eyes loomed into view. She was face to face with a Golden Diving Bell spider!

CHAPTER NINETEEN

'L et me go!' squealed Lana.

'Good one,' said the Golden Diving Bell spider with a hearty chuckle, as if she had made a particularly funny joke. His fur

seemed to be *much* tuftier than hers, sticking up in a giant quiff just above his middle four eyes, and his face was oddly familiar.

'Every spider in this marsh has to leave, right now!'

'Nice try,' said the spider. 'But I know what you girl spiders are like, thanks very much.'

'What do you mean?' asked Lana indignantly.

'You eat us!' exclaimed the spider. 'I've heard the stories. The second I let you go, you'll bite me, wrap me in thread, inject me with your digestive juices, then suck me up like a smoothie. My mother always told me, if a girl spider comes into your nest, don't ask questions, just bundle her up and get out of there as fast as your eight legs will carry you.'

'Let me out of here!' insisted Lana, struggling helplessly against her bonds. 'You can't say that about *all* girls.'

'You're not going anywhere,' said the spider. 'Not unless you guess the riddle.'

'What riddle?' asked Lana.

The spider tipped his head away, giving Lana the equivalent of four side-eyes. 'Are you tricking me? Every spider has a riddle. You guess it, you go free.'

Lana stared at him blankly.

'Mine is really hard to guess, though.' The spider puffed out his chest proudly. 'Want to hear it?'

'I *want* you to let me go,' replied Lana.

'Okay,' said the spider, preparing himself. 'In the winter I go naked, in the summer I wear clothes, I breathe out what you breathe in and burn red hot when it snows.'

'What?' asked Lana. 'Say that again.'

'Uh-uh,' said the spider, shaking his head. 'You know the rules. You only get to hear it once.'

'I have no idea.'

'A tree!' crowed the spider gleefully. 'Get it? It's naked in the winter because it loses its leaves. It breathes out oxygen, which we breathe in. And it gets burnt as logs when it's cold outside. I told you it was a good one.' He grinned.

'What's your name?' asked Lana, changing tack.

'Elvis,' replied the spider warily. 'Why?'

'After Elvis Presley?' asked Lana, in surprise. 'The famous singer?' Now she knew where she had seen that hair before.

'Never heard of him.'

'He's my nana's favourite,' said Lana. 'She plays his songs all the time. There's a poster of him on my bedroom wall.'

The spider raised his two front legs in what looked like a shrug.

'Doesn't matter. Can I be honest with you?' asked Lana, holding his gaze. 'I'm not really a spider.'

'Okay . . .' said Elvis hesitantly.

Lana took a breath, then said carefully, 'I'm a human.'

There was a pause, then Elvis pulled a disgusted face. 'Eww, yuck! A human?' He spat saliva out from between his jaws, as if he was trying to get rid of a nasty taste. 'Ugh! Why would you say that? Humans are disgusting!'

'What?' asked Lana. 'No, they're not!'

'The way they move,' said Elvis, screwing up his face. 'It gives me the creeps. Two legs!' He raised himself up on his two hind legs and imitated a human walk. 'Wobbling all over the place. Like any second, they're going to fall over and squish you flat. And that weird liquid they have on their skin! It's like something from a nightmare!'

'You mean sweat?' asked Lana, so fascinated she had forgotten what a dreadful hurry she was in.

'A drop fell in this pond once.' Elvis grimaced, placing a foot to his mouth delicately. 'Stank like snail sick. I had to rush up out of the water and hurl on the bank. Plus, humans have got no fangs! I mean, how weird is that? Just little pink fleshy holes with weird stubby white bones poking out. It makes me queasy just thinking about it.'

'Spiders look pretty weird too,' countered Lana.

'Two eyes!' exclaimed Elvis, ignoring her. 'How do they see anything? And those weird wrinkly funnels on the sides of their head they listen with! And no fur, except for that small patch on the top of their head. I mean, you couldn't make it up. It's like someone set out to think up the most bizarre-looking creature on the planet, then didn't know when to stop. Just don't get in their way, that's my advice. Stone-cold killers. Don't care about any other animal except themselves.'

'Exactly!' exclaimed Lana, triumphantly, suddenly remembering her mission. 'We're in their way right now! We have to get out of here, all of us. They're going to wipe out the marsh!'

The spider frowned, then burst into laughter.

'Wipe out the marsh! I love it. I mean, I've got to hand it to you, you're putting everything into this –' his eyes narrowed and his voice changed – '. . . subterfuge.'

'I don't know what that means,' said Lana.

'Deception,' explained the spider. 'You're trying to make me think we're in danger, so that I'll untie you and you can eat me!'

'It's not a trick!' exclaimed Lana. 'I promise you. I'm a human. I ate a magic berry that a bear gave me, to turn me into a spider, so I could warn you all!'

There was a long silence.

'Okay, then,' said Elvis. 'Why would the humans want to wipe out the marsh?'

'To build houses. For humans.'

The spider widened all eight of his eyes. 'Seriously?' he asked. 'Surely not even humans could be that cruel. *Or* that stupid! Even if they don't care about spiders, think of all the other species that live here: the plants, the birds, the insects, the fish! I mean, we all need each other, don't we? To survive?'

'Trust me,' said Lana. 'That's what they're going to do. They're out there now!'

'But that's crazy!' Elvis gave her a long, hard stare, his black eyes gleaming. 'You know what my granny used to say?'

Lana didn't.

'"Nature, Elvis, is like a web. Every living thing is connected."'

There was a long pause, while the spider considered his next move.

'Okay, then,' he said finally. 'But if you eat me after all this, I'm going to be really cross.'

He edged forward cautiously, pulling a bunch of threads towards his jaws and snipping it through.

Then he stopped.

'What's the matter?' asked Lana.

'Can you feel that?'

But Lana, who was still dangling from the roof, couldn't feel anything.

'There it is again! The ground is shaking!'

The sole of a giant work boot came crashing down towards them, and a vicious current hurled Lana and Elvis out of the golden nest, into the cloudy waters of the marsh!

CHAPTER TWENTY

For several horrible seconds, Lana tumbled through the water, trussed up like a Sunday chicken, with no idea which way was up or down. She felt her body squirm, as it searched for air to breathe, but no air came. Then, just when she was about to pass out completely, she felt herself being dragged up out of the water and into the shallows at the edge of the marsh.

'You were telling the truth!' blurted Elvis.

'What?' gasped Lana, struggling to catch her breath.

'Humans!' declared the spider, pointing with three of his legs, for emphasis. Peering through the grass, Lana spotted a spray of woodchips as the workman continued to saw away at the base of the Hollow Tree. She scowled, more furious than ever that Carl had tricked her into believing he would save her magnificent friend. How could she have been so *stupid*?

As the two spiders watched, the giant Carl leaned forward and tapped the worker on the shoulder. 'Hurry up!' he shouted. 'We haven't got all day.' Beside him, the other two workers nudged each other, enjoying the moment.

The worker shut off the saw and removed his ear protectors. 'Everything okay, boss?'

'Give those to me,' snapped Carl, holding out his hand.

The worker sheepishly handed over his ear protectors, gloves and saw.

'Watch and learn,' declared Carl, firing up the saw and turning it to maximum power. As its teeth bit into the soft bark, the ground beneath them began to shake.

'They're cutting it down!' yelped Elvis.

'And look!' warned Lana, pointing across the marsh. 'See those big yellow machines? And that huge pile of gravel? As soon as the tree's gone, they're going to fill all of this in!'

'Right,' said Elvis, plunging back into the water. 'I'm releasing my hormone!'

If spiders had eyebrows, Lana would have frowned. 'Your hormone? What's that?'

'Instant messaging,' explained Elvis. 'For spiders.'

Lana glanced down at her eight feet, which were still submerged in the water. They were tingling with pleasure! As she watched, a warm glow chased up through her legs to her body, where it fizzed and sparkled!

'Ooh!' she blurted in delight.

'Good, isn't it?' asked Elvis.

Behind him, two new spiders emerged from the water. 'Elvis,' said one anxiously. 'What gives?'

'Eustace, Constance, meet Lana,' said Elvis. 'It's an emergency, and she's in charge!'

The water around them began to shift, as if a large net was surfacing. But it wasn't a net, it was the legs of dozens and dozens of spiders!

'Quickly, everyone!' exclaimed Lana, as countless eyes emerged from the water. 'Humans are attacking the marsh!'

The spiders broke into excited chatter.

'*Sssh*, everyone, please!' shouted Lana. 'Somewhere here is a thread that will lead us all to safety. Could everyone take a couple of steps back? Thank you!'

The sea of spiders retreated. Sure enough, there was her golden thread, still attached to the pebble.

'Got it!' she shouted. 'Follow me!'

Without a moment's delay, Lana began hauling herself along the thread, hurdling leaves, leaping twigs and skittering over puddles as wide as lakes. Glancing back, her heart leaped when she saw Elvis doing the same. He was followed by a lengthy string of spiders, rattling along like beads on a necklace.

But her good feelings were short-lived. Up ahead, the teeth of the chainsaw were already heading for the corner of the Hollow Tree's mouth!

'Faster!' she hissed. 'We have to go faster!'

'Faster!' hissed Elvis to the spider behind him. 'We have to go faster!'

'Faster! We have to go faster!' repeated the next spider. The message travelled all the way down the line, finally reaching the spider that was last but one. 'Parsnips!' he announced importantly to the very last spider. *'We need to buy parsnips!'*

But it was too late. Lana watched in horror as the chainsaw chewed through the last fragment of bark, lurching forward into the Hollow Tree's open mouth and slicing right through their golden thread!

Lana toppled backwards, landing heavily on Elvis, who fell onto the spider behind him. Then, one by one, every spider in the line found themselves flat on their bottoms.

'Hey, get off me!' squeaked the spider at the back. 'Hey, get off me!' squeaked the spider in front of him, then the next, all the way back up the line to Elvis. 'Hay-flavoured toffee!' he squeaked enthusiastically, then considered his words. 'Sorry,' he said. 'That doesn't make any sense.'

But Lana was too deep in thought to mind. They needed a new plan, and fast!

'You're the leader now,' she said to Elvis, releasing the golden thread. 'Aim for the eye socket, the one furthest from the saw, and take this lot with you.'

'But where are you going?' asked Elvis.

'Trust me,' said Lana. 'You don't want to know.' Elvis nodded slowly.

'Got it,' he said. 'See you on the other side.' He turned to the spider next to him. 'Follow me!' he urged. 'Pass it on!'

'Follow me!' said the spider to his neighbour. 'Pass it on!' Once again, the message reached the last spider in the line. 'Naomi! Arthur's gone!' he yelled. Then added, 'Wait . . . who's Naomi?'

Lana, meanwhile, was bounding up the laces of Carl's work boot to where his woolly sock met his bare shin. Stretching up above her was a cliff face of wrinkled pink flesh, disappearing into the darkness of his shorts. She swallowed hard, summoning all her courage.

As she watched, a giant globule of sweat avalanched down, narrowly missing her, before crashing into the towelling fibres of Carl's sock. A whiff, somewhere between fungus and old cheese, took to the breeze. Lana made a face. Elvis was right: seen from a spider's point of view, humans were gross.

But this was no time for squeamishness. She had to stop the sawing before it was too late.

Leaping from hair to hair, she began to make

her way up Carl's sweaty shin. He was rocking back and forth as he sawed through the tree, so she had to carefully time her run up his thigh to match the precise moment the canvas of his shorts leg was hanging loose. Holding her breath, she was soon crossing the pongy seat of his underpants and squeezing out of the fetid gap between his leather belt and the small of his back. From there, she headed upwards, only to find herself log-fluming back down a river of putrid sweat. At the last moment she gripped his belt, leaving her dangling in mid-air, the ground swinging far beneath her.

Switching tactics, she clung to the inside of Carl's shirt and began to climb. Emerging at his collar, she shimmied up the stubble on his neck, over his cheek and onto the end of his nose.

'See?' shouted Carl, showing off. 'This is how you cut down a tree!'

As he made his boast, he turned, bringing himself face to face with his three workers.

'Err . . . boss,' said one of them, pointing at her own nose. 'I think you might have something here.'

'Can't hear you!' shouted Carl.

'SPIDER!' yelled the worker, making a movement in the air with her hand.

Shaking his head in irritation, Carl shut off the saw and snatched off his ear protectors.

'What?' he demanded. Then he felt it: a ticklish sensation on the end of his nose.

Lana shifted her position slightly. Looking down, she saw that Carl was holding the saw directly over a deep puddle. This was her chance!

She bit into his flesh, hard.

CHAPTER TWENTY-ONE

'YEEAAARRGGGHHH!!!!!!'
bawled Carl. *SPLASH!* went the saw,
landing in the muddy water and
sinking quickly out of sight. 'EEE—AAAHH—
OWW!' screeched Carl, as he tried desperately
to brush away the spider that had just bitten the
end of his nose.

But Lana had vanished.

'Where's it gone?' yelped Carl.

'Over here!' yelled the first worker, clouting Carl's left ear so hard his teeth rattled.

'YEEE-OW!' protested Carl.

'Now it's here!' bellowed another, slapping Carl's other ear.

'OOW! Stop it!'

'It's back again!' The third worker gleefully walloped the first ear again.

'I said OOOOW!'

But Lana was already parachuting to the floor from a thread she had attached to Carl's earlobe. Just as she was about to hit the ground, she stopped spooling thread, bouncing like an unravelled yo-yo before snipping herself free with her razor-sharp jaws. She wasn't out of danger yet, though. As she chased through the reeds, heading for the mouth of the Hollow Tree, Carl's voice boomed out above her.

'There it is!' he roared. 'Get it!'

His shadow loomed over her and Lana glanced up to see his enormous work boot crashing down towards her!

She put on a burst of speed, his boot landing heavily in the mud immediately behind her. Changing direction, she headed for a nearby stretch of water, hoping to dive for cover, but Carl's yellow hard hat came plunging down on top of her, trapping her underneath!

'Help!' screamed Lana, racing from one side of the hat to another, looking desperately for a way out. 'Help!'

Suddenly, the hat flew up into the air, revealing Carl's giant pink face. A red bite was swelling on the tip of his bulging nose.

'Got you!' he boomed, and Lana saw his giant glove plunging towards her.

This was it – she was going to be squished. But as his fist came crashing down, she felt a loop of thread tighten around her waist, yanking her to safety! Elvis had come to the rescue.

'Come on!' he yelled, snipping her free, before leading her up through a maze of channels in the bark, into the nose-hole of the Hollow Tree.

As they ran, another colossal boot crashed down just centimetres behind them and the three workers' voices vibrated like foghorns.

'Did I get it?' said one, peering down at her footprint. 'I think I got it.'

'Spiders,' said another. 'The sooner we fill this marsh in the better.'

'Thanks,' gasped Lana as soon she and Elvis were safely inside the tree.

'I'm the one who's grateful,' replied Elvis. 'Look,' he said, pointing up the hollow.

Lana peered upwards, her eyes adjusting to the dark. The storm was still raging at the top of the tree and lightning flashed in the circle of sky above her. The inside of the hollow was carpeted in spiders, hurrying upwards in search of freedom. A wave of joy swept over her. She'd done it! She'd saved them!

Well, *almost*. Glancing back, she saw one of the workers pulling and re-pulling the starter cord of the drenched petrol saw, which spluttered sadly.

'It's broken,' he boomed.

'Call the supplier,' ordered Carl. 'And get another one.'

'No point.' The workman shrugged. 'They don't open until nine.'

'That's three hours from now!' exclaimed Carl, rubbing the back of his neck in frustration. 'The whole idea was to cut it down before anyone woke up.'

Lana beamed at Elvis, who grinned right back. Three hours might be just enough to rescue Harrison and get back again! 'Quick!' she shouted. 'Let's get out of here while we still can!'

Feeling a surge of energy, she flittered up the inside of the hollow, joining the sea of jostling spiders as they edged their way upwards. The crowd had a mind of its own, and she was soon swept this way and that, separated from Elvis.

But her excitement soon turned to fear. As she reached the top, lightning flashed again and a clap of thunder rang out, so loud it sounded as if the sky was splitting. A violent wind was raging, hurling snowflakes the size of mattresses and shaking the Hollow Tree's giant branches as easily as if they were skipping ropes.

Lana watched in wonder as one by one each spider reached the top of the tree. They bowed their heads and raised their bodies, then flung trails of thread into the air, which carried them away like hot-air balloons!

'Hey!' she called. 'Where are you guys going?'

As she spoke, a spider clambered up beside her. 'Coming, Your Majesty!' he yelled.

'Your Majesty?' echoed Lana.

'Wheeeeee!' replied the spider, taking off on the wind.

The wind picked up once more and Lana had to clutch the bark with all eight of her feet to stop herself being blown away.

'Breathe it in!' called a familiar voice. 'That's the smell of adventure!'

It was Elvis! Perched high on a neighbouring branch, his quiff danced in the wind!

'Breathe what in?' echoed Lana.

'Are you not getting that?' asked Elvis. He closed his eyes and inhaled deeply. 'There's only one spider on Earth makes a scent like that. The queen!'

Lana let the wind chase over her, bristling through the hairs on her legs. Her whole body began to tingle, just like it had in the marsh.

'She's calling us,' explained Elvis.

Lana's eyes snapped open. This was it: her chance to find Harrison!

'Here I come, Your Majesty!' bawled another spider, taking off on the wind. Lana watched as the breeze carried him higher and higher towards the clouds.

'Elvis, wait!' she called. 'What do I do?'

'It's called ballooning,' explained Elvis. 'It's how we spiders get around. All you need is some thread and a steady breeze! Throw your weight forward onto your front legs, so that your body is pointing upwards. Then the next time you feel a big gust, fire out a few strands of silk. The next thing you know, you'll be sipping caterpillar smoothies with Her Majesty herself.'

Another gust whistled past and Elvis let go of the bark, shooting upwards into the churning sky.

As Lana stood at the top of the Hollow Tree,

looking out across the frozen forest, her heart soared with hope. All she needed to do was join the squadron of flying spiders, and they'd lead her right to the Spider Queen's lair! If King Yashar was right, that meant she'd soon find her brother!

Summoning all her strength, she leaned forward onto her front legs and released a short strand of thread. It shot straight up in the air, tugging at her abdomen like a helium balloon, but the force wasn't nearly enough to lift her.

Beside her, more and more spiders were taking off. She noticed that their threads were much longer than hers, and there were more of them. After firing out another short strand, she focused all her concentration on shooting out several long streamers. The tree fell away beneath her as she was lifted into the air! Higher and higher she flew, until the snow-covered clearing was no more than the size of a pocket handkerchief.

Flying high above the ridge, she saw the canyon open beneath her. It was still in the grip of a terrible storm. Thunder rolled out across the sky, as dark clouds swirled above the lake, spitting forks of lightning at the village.

Suddenly, on the slope below her, she spotted four familiar figures: the Warden and his three guards, searching a bank of gorse bushes. All four were drenched. Their horses were laden with everything from blankets to pots and pans, as if they had left the village in a hurry.

Curious, she steered herself down towards them.

As she drew closer, she saw the Warden point at something in the bushes.

'Here it is!' he announced proudly. 'We can shelter here until the storm has passed.'

It was the bear's cave! Pulling on the threads,

Lana circled above them, listening in on their conversation.

'I knew this place would come in handy,' said the Warden, swinging down from his horse.

'But, Sire,' said one of his henchmen. 'What about the villagers?'

'Trust me,' replied the Warden. 'There won't *be* a village after this storm. It's every man for himself now.'

Lana was disgusted. The Warden and his guards had abandoned the villagers to the storm and were planning to hide out in the bear's cave! Pulling on the threads again, she steered upwards to re-join the stream of Golden Diving Bell spiders, all of them gleefully riding the wind.

'Lana!' called a familiar voice, and once again she found herself next to Elvis, riding a warmer current of air. 'I thought I'd lost you!'

'I'm fine,' replied Lana.

They were now in sight of the village. It was in the grip of a violent gale. Several huts had collapsed, and Lana could see terrified villagers scurrying around like ants. Looking ahead, she caught sight of a vapour trail of ballooning spiders, heading far out over the windswept lake, then curving down towards its surface.

'Where's she taking us?' she called out to Elvis.

'Who?' asked Elvis, throwing what looked like karate moves as he rode the wind.

'The Spider Queen! Where's her palace?'

'Under there,' he replied, indicating the lake, as if it was the most obvious answer in the world. 'Where else?'

Of course! thought Lana. *It's been under the lake all along. No wonder King Yashar couldn't find it!* But before she could reply, she was blown sideways by a powerful gust of wind. Giant raindrops hurtled past, some of them bigger than she was.

'Lana!' called Elvis, veering upwards. 'You're flying too low!'

'I'll see you at the palace!' called Lana. 'I have to help my friends!'

Pulling on the threads again, she brought herself lower and lower, dodging the raindrops, making a beeline for the village. As she flew over the stockade wall, Lana saw the bear, locked in the stocks. Beyond him, Gudrun and a group of villagers were trying to lift a fallen hut. Steeling her nerves, she swooped down and made a crash-landing in the bear's left ear.

'King Yashar!' she called. 'It's me, Lana!'

She felt the bear's head move from side to side, as if he was searching for the owner of the small squeaky voice.

'I'm a spider, and I'm in your ear!'

'Lana!' boomed Yashar. 'So, the purple berry came in handy after all. Quick, set me free! Gudrun's hut collapsed and Kyle is trapped inside.'

'Set you free? How?'

'There's a latch, here to my right. All you need to do is unhitch it.'

As fast as she could, Lana scurried out of the bear's ear, down his sodden neck, onto the rough-hewn wood of the stocks. Moments later, she arrived at the latch: a giant iron hook and eye. She attached a strand of thread to the hook and began to climb, hoping to pull it free.

But the weight was far too much for her. As the thread drew tight, her legs buckled and her feet began to slip and slide. Gasping with exhaustion, she returned to the bear's ear.

'I'm not strong enough!' protested Lana.

'What about the green berry I gave you?' asked the bear. 'The one that gives you strength. Do you still have it?'

'No,' said Lana sadly. 'I lost it.'

'What?' asked the bear, his voice sharp with frustration. 'Where?'

'In the Great Hall, when I was waiting for the Spider Queen. It fell between the floorboards and I couldn't get it out. The gap was too small.'

'For a human, perhaps. But not for a spider. Fetch it, quick!'

Needing no further encouragement, Lana clambered down onto the stocks, and fired three strands of thread into the air, taking off in the direction of the Great Hall. Below her, she glimpsed Gudrun and some of the villagers, struggling to lift a heavy beam.

'Kyle!' called Gudrun, in panic. 'Kyle!'

The bear was right. Kyle was in danger. There was no time to lose!

Moments later, Lana landed beside the skylight, high on the roof of the Great Hall. Anchoring a thread, she abseiled down into the darkness, landing neatly on the floorboards. There she circled round and round until she found the green berry, wedged deep in the gap. Piercing its thick skin with her jaws, she then began to suck, drawing in the sweet-tasting juice. As soon as her stomach was full, she climbed back up the thread and took flight once again to land beside the latch.

This time, lifting it was easy. The instant the hook rattled free, she scampered back to the bear's ear in triumph.

'Your Majesty!' she called. 'You're free. Go and save Kyle – then come and find me!'

'Find you?' asked the bear. 'Where?'

'You see those dots up there?' She felt the bear's head tilt upwards. 'Those are spiders. Follow them: they're heading to the Spider Queen's underwater palace. And I'm going to join them!'

Climbing onto the top of the bear's ear, she fired more threads, and the wind took her up again to join the swarm. She just had time to see King Yashar lift the beam, freeing Kyle, before she found herself plunging down towards the angry waters, diving deep below the surface, bubbles once again clinging to the tiny hairs that lined her body.

And then she saw it.

She and all the other spiders were heading down towards an enormous golden palace, just below the surface of the lake.

CHAPTER TWENTY-TWO

Down Lana dived, one spider among many, swimming towards the palace. She saw now that the building was in the shape of a giant spider, with a head, body and eight legs. A trail of bubbles rose above it, breaking on the surface of the lake. She guessed they must contain the Spider Queen's hormone.

So, this was where the Spider Queen lived!

She swam on, flocking with her comrades,

The building was in the shape of a giant spider

heading for the mouth of the building.

Soon she was hauling herself up onto the golden floor of a large entrance chamber, which she realized must make up the spider's head. Everywhere she looked, the Golden Diving Bell spiders from the marsh were shaking themselves dry, chattering and heading towards an archway at the far end of the room.

A line of Greeting Spiders in gold tabards were handing out golden sheets of paper. One smiled and said, 'Welcome to the Palace of the Spider Queen. Here's your orientation pack.'

'My what?' asked Lana.

'Orientation pack. It'll help you get settled in. The queen is in the Great Chamber,' said the spider, pointing towards the archway. 'Hurry, or you'll miss her speech. She has a very important announcement to make.'

Lana glanced around, hoping to see Elvis, but there was no sign of him.

Now that she saw so many spiders up close, it was plainer than ever that they all had different faces and personalities, just like humans. How could she ever have thought that all spiders were the same?

Lana followed a large crowd through the archway into the Great Chamber, the reflections of the spiders magnified by the gold of the walls.

At the far end of the room, the Spider Queen, now in human form, was standing on a golden platform. With the fingers of one hand, she was touching the distinctive golden necklace around her neck, as her other hand traced elaborate shapes in the air. Lana knew instantly that she was casting some sort of spell.

'What's she doing?' she whispered to the spider next to her.

'No idea,' replied the spider, who was wearing a multicoloured woollen hat. 'I'm just a humble greenfly herder from the mountains. But it looks important.'

'She's summoning a storm,' explained a spider with a large moustache. 'To destroy the humans' village.'

That answer jolted Lana back to reality. The spiders might be good, but their queen most definitely was not.

She saw now that there were eight passages leading off the Great Chamber. One of them must lead to Harrison. Looking around to make sure she wasn't being watched, she edged towards the nearest entrance, then scurried down it.

She bumped straight into an elderly spider with four walking sticks coming the other way. 'Looking for someone?' he asked.

'No,' said Lana, shaking her head. Was it her imagination, or was her vision blurring?

'Two minutes to the queen's speech,' he hissed. 'Don't be late.'

'I won't,' she said, crossing two of her legs behind her back to protect her from her own lie, and continued on down the passage.

But as she ran, desperately looking for signs of Harrison, she started to feel more and more lightheaded. Running in a straight line became almost impossible and she found herself veering crazily, bouncing from wall to wall. Feeling a cramping in her chest, she rolled over onto her back, curling her legs up into a ball. Then everything vanished into blackness.

The first thing she saw when she woke was a human hand, pressed hard against her face.

It took a few moments before she realized it was her own.

Frowning, she pushed herself up into a seated position and looked around. She was still in the empty corridor.

The purple berry! she remembered, jolting back to reality. *The one that turned me into a spider. It must have worn off!*

Balancing on two legs seemed almost impossible after being used to eight, but somehow Lana managed it, placing one hand on the smooth gold wall for occasional support as she staggered to the end of the corridor. How had she managed before with such a huge, clumsy body?

At the end of the corridor was an enormous bedroom, with all the furniture made of gold.

There was a golden bed with golden silk sheets and pillows, a golden dressing table with a golden chair and mirror, and a golden clothes rack with lots of golden capes hanging on it.

Frowning, Lana glanced in the mirror. Sure enough, she was back in her human form, her hair messy and her clothes spattered with mud. How would the spiders react to having a human other than their queen in their midst?

Moments later there was a tiny scream, and she had her answer. Peering round, she could just make out a tiny spider in a maid's uniform, who had arrived in the entrance and was backing away in fear.

'Don't be scared!' called Lana.

But the spider was already scurrying away, back down the corridor. Lana needed to act fast, before she had a chance to raise the alarm. Quick as a flash, she grabbed an empty water glass from the Spider Queen's bedside table, raced back down the corridor, and placed it over the running spider.

'Sorry!' whispered Lana, over the sound of tiny, muffled squeals. 'I'll set you free as soon as I can, I promise! Only right now I have to rescue my brother.'

Luckily for Lana, back in the Great Chamber the lights were dimming, ready for the Spider Queen to begin her speech, and all her subjects were gathered in rapt attention.

'Greetings!' boomed the queen.

As she spoke, Lana tiptoed round the edge of the auditorium.

'Welcome,' began the queen, surveying the spiders far below her, 'to our brothers and sisters from the marsh, who had a narrow escape this afternoon from some particularly unpleasant humans . . .'

Frowning, Lana scanned the seven remaining corridors, trying to figure out which one might lead to the larder that King Yashar had told her about. But they all looked the same. Just as she was losing hope, she spotted a small group of spiders in chef hats taking their seats at the far side of the auditorium. The corridor they were emerging from must lead to a kitchen! Where else but a kitchen would you expect to find a larder?

'For too long,' continued the Spider Queen, 'we spiders have been terrorized by our two-legged enemies. Now that is going to change!'

A cheer went up from the assembled spiders, and Lana saw her chance. Crawling on all fours, so as not to be seen from the stage, she scuttled round the back of the auditorium, launching herself into the corridor that she had seen the chef spiders exiting. Moments later she found herself in a large empty kitchen. Throwing open the other doors, she found a spice cupboard, a treasure trove of pots and pans, and finally the larder.

Golden shelves lined the room, and on each lay a human-sized cocoon. Heart pounding, Lana tiptoed closer to the nearest of them. The golden webbing encasing the villager was skin-tight, and she could just make out the features of the person inside. He seemed to be fast asleep with his eyes closed, a simple crown sitting high on his forehead. Lana gasped. She was face to face with King Yashar's brother, Prince Zephir!

She searched the other cocoons, but they all belonged to grown-ups. Then finally, on a low shelf at the back, she found what she was looking for: a cocoon the size of a twelve-year-old boy.

'Harrison?' she whispered.

But the cocoon didn't move. Lana felt her breath catch in her throat. *Was he all right?*

'Harrison!' she cried, shaking him by the shoulders. But there was no response. 'Harrison, wake up!'

'Lana?' came a sleepy voice. 'Is that you?'

'I've come to save you!' hissed Lana, flooded with relief. 'Are you okay?'

'Would you leave me alone, please?' murmured Harrison, rolling over. 'I'm trying to get some sleep.'

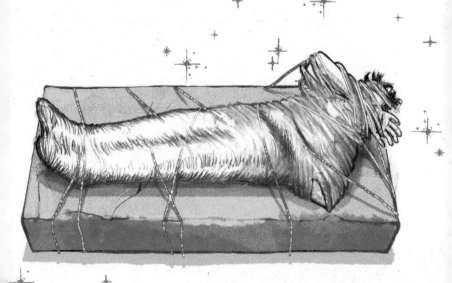

'Harrison,' she whispered gently. 'It's time to get up.'

Summoning every ounce of strength the green berry had given her, she began to prise apart the golden threads that encased her brother. Even with the bear's magic to help her, it was still a struggle. But finally, sweaty and exhausted, she snapped the final strands and shook him awake.

'Where am I?' murmured Harrison sleepily.

'The Spider Queen's palace,' said Lana.

Harrison looked at her in groggy confusion.

'Who's the Spider Queen?' he asked.

Lana raised her eyebrows. 'You're about to find out.'

CHAPTER TWENTY-THREE

'Are you with me?' the Spider Queen roared, prowling the brightly lit stage, scouring the multitude of excited spiders crowding the slopes of the Great Chamber. 'Are you ready to fight back?'

'Yes! We! Are!' answered the horde as one. A group of young spiders at one end of the seating area reared up, raising their front legs in an attempt to start a Mexican wave, but it soon petered out.

'Or will you stand by?' bellowed the queen. 'And let them destroy our homes, our families and our futures?'

'No! We! Will! Not!' replied the spiders.

'It is time for each and every one of us to stand up and be counted!' growled the queen.

'Death to all humans!' squeaked one particularly angry spider in the front row.

Once again, the young spiders tried to start a Mexican wave and this time everyone joined in. It travelled right round the room and almost all the way back again, washing up at the feet of the young spiders who had started it, as the entire auditorium burst into applause.

'Tonight,' announced the queen triumphantly, 'we are going to finish what we started. No human can say we didn't warn them!'

'True! True!' cried the spiders.

'We began with kidnappings. But did they listen? No. We sent storms! They ignored those too. Gales! Blizzards! Every message went unheeded. Now, finally, with this deadly tempest, they have met their reckoning. Soon the lake will be ours and ours alone!'

At that, Lana stepped out of the shadows towards the stage.

'No,' she said, in as clear and strong a voice as she could muster. 'What you are doing is wrong.'

A spotlight swished away from the queen, searching for Lana in the darkness. As it struck its target, a hush fell over the room, as every spider in the audience scuttled round to fix this strange new human with all eight of its eyes.

The Spider Queen fixed Lana with an icy stare. 'So,' she breathed. 'Here you are at last.' Then turning to her audience, she said calmly, 'I brought this girl here to teach her a lesson. Let's see if she has learned it.'

'Put her in the larder!' piped up the angry spider in the front row, and the room erupted. Some spiders whooped and jeered, others chattered excitedly and one or two even screamed in terror

at the sight of what they considered to be an abomination of nature.

'Silence,' instructed the queen, spreading her hands in a commanding gesture, and the din swiftly subsided. Then, raising one elegant eyebrow, she returned her attention to Lana.

'Come, girl,' she beckoned with a bony finger. 'And join me on the stage.'

Hesitantly, Lana stepped up onto the smooth golden stage, aware that countless eyes were watching her from the darkness of the auditorium.

'Well?' asked the queen, in a voice so cold her words seemed to freeze in the air. 'Tell us what you have learned.'

Lana took a deep breath. 'I used to think,' she began, her

voice trembling with emotion, 'that people were more important than spiders.'

'Execute her!' screeched the angry spider on the front row, and once again, the audience erupted.

'Silence!' bellowed the queen, pointing at the angry little spider.

'Sorry, Your Majesty,' he said meekly. 'I've never been to one of these things before, and I got a bit carried away.'

'Speak,' instructed the queen, gesturing for Lana to continue.

'The last time we met,' said Lana, steeling herself, 'someone asked me if I would prefer spiders or an adventure playground. And I chose an adventure playground.'

The spider at the front opened his mouth to speak, then caught the queen's eye and thought better of it.

'It was selfish. I was only thinking of myself and the fun I would have.'

One or two spiders in the front row crossed their front legs. Others tutted and shook their heads. Her talk was going down badly, but Lana battled on.

'The truth is, back then, I didn't really care about other creatures. Not all of them. I mean, I liked unicorns and pandas and koala bears and cute things like that. But spiders . . .' Lana hesitated, wondering whether she should say the thought that was in her mind. 'I thought they were ugly and scary.'

The audience gasped. 'Harrison was different,' she said quickly, turning to where her brother lurked in the shadows.

'Look out!' shrieked an elderly spider at the back, seeing Harrison for the first time. 'There's another one!'

Once again, the room echoed with excitement, shock and horror. But Lana pressed on. 'He thought all creatures were equal. But not me.'

There was a murmur of agreement.

'But coming here,' continued Lana, 'and meeting all of you, has changed all that. I've learned that spiders have thoughts, and feelings, and hopes and dreams just like humans do. And that to you guys, humans look strange!'

'It's true!' shouted a voice in the crowd. It was Elvis!

A spotlight picked him out, and every spider in the room watched as he made his way towards the stage.

'To us, humans look really weird,' he confirmed, pushing back his quiff with one of his front legs. 'And the way they move is so creepy.' Raising himself up on his two hind legs to demonstrate, he staggered across the stage to join Lana. 'I mean, what's with those two upper legs? They're so weedy they can't even walk on them! But that's all on the outside. It's what's on the inside that counts. And this human here . . . Her inside is brimming with kindness. She cares – really cares – about spiders. She risked her life to save us. But don't just take my word for it. Stand up if you're from the marshes!' he bellowed.

One by one, nearly a hundred spiders stood up, spread right across the hall.

'Yes, I know she's strange-looking,' Elvis continued. 'And boy, up close like this, it's even more intense. But she's not our enemy!' he exclaimed. 'She's our friend!'

'Lana! Lana!' the marsh spiders in the audience began to chant.

Once again, the Spider Queen raised her hands to silence them.

'Very well, girl,' she declared, rounding on Lana. 'If you're our friend, why try to sabotage my plan?'

'Because humans and spiders don't have to destroy one another! They can learn to be friends.'

'She's got a point!' called Elvis, and the spiders around him muttered their agreement.

'Your Majesty,' said Lana, appealing to the Spider Queen. 'The humans in this village – they don't know their nets are destroying your homes. But maybe we can explain that to them. And find a way to live together.'

'Live together?' repeated the queen disbelievingly. 'How do you propose to do that?'

'What if we move the humans' village? And ask them not to fish for oysters in your part of the lake?'

'Ha!' laughed the Spider Queen scornfully. 'How utterly, miraculously, stupendously, pointlessly foolish of you. Humans can't be trusted! They are killing machines, pure and simple. They can't live in harmony with each other, let alone animals.'

Excited chatter broke out among the spiders again.

'But this isn't the answer!' protested Lana. 'Breaking up families. Wrecking homes, kidnapping my brother! It's as bad as anything the humans are doing.' Then, seeing the look of determination in the Spider Queen's eyes, Lana turned to the audience. 'You see that, don't you?' she appealed to them. 'You see that what she's doing is wrong?'

A ripple of confusion swept across the Great Chamber. Perhaps sensing that she was losing her grip, the Spider Queen drew herself up to her full height and declared, 'I think we've heard enough. It's time you and your brother joined your friends in the larder.'

'Wait!' called a lone voice from the front, clear and commanding. Persuaded by Lana's argument, the angry little spider was experiencing a change of heart! 'The riddle! Let her answer the riddle!'

CHAPTER TWENTY-FOUR

'The riddle?' asked Lana. 'What's that?'

'I told you,' whispered Elvis. 'Every spider has a riddle! But the riddle of the Spider Queen is special. Answer it correctly and you become queen in her place.'

'The riddle! The riddle!' chanted the spiders.

'Impossible!' roared the queen. 'She's a human, not a spider! The rules don't apply!'

'Put it to a vote!' called Elvis, and the entire hall

murmured in agreement. 'If you, our queen, are the worthier challenger, you will prevail!'

'Who here believes the girl should answer my riddle?' The queen glared.

For a few anxious moments, no spider dared defy its monarch. Then Elvis bravely raised one of his front legs. The angry spider at the front joined him, and one by one every spider in the hall voted in favour!

'Very well,' spat the queen. 'Answer it correctly, and you shall have my golden necklace, seat of all my powers, and become queen of the spiders in my place!'

There was instant uproar.

'But if she fails . . .' The Spider Queen held up her hand for quiet. 'She goes in the larder with her brother and we dash the village to smithereens!'

Elvis caught Lana's eye, willing her to succeed.

'Now, silence!' ordered the queen. 'While I conjure something truly fiendish.'

All the spiders watched as the queen paced across the stage, racking her brains. Once or twice, a suitable brainteaser formed on her lips, only for her to discard it as being too easy. To defeat this challenger, she needed a truly impossible conundrum.

Feeling a hand in hers, Lana turned to see Harrison beside her on the stage. He managed a warm smile, despite his wooziness, and Lana felt her spirits lift.

'I am ready to pose the question,' declared the queen at last, a cruel smile playing across her lips. 'Girl, are you sure you wish to answer? It's not too late to change your mind.'

Lana nodded. 'I'm sure,' she said loudly.

'Very well. Listen carefully, for I am duty bound

to say this only once. The riddle I pose is this . . .'

A hush fell over the Great Chamber. Somewhere at the back, a trendy-looking spider with thick red glasses gave an excited yelp, and was immediately hushed by its neighbour.

'I'm stronger than steel and softer than silk, drier than dust and wetter than milk, I hide in the summer and show in the frost, as soon as you fight me the battle is lost.'

Lana's face fell. How could something be strong and soft? Or dry and wet?

'Any ideas?' she asked Harrison under her breath.

'None at all,' replied Harrison, shrugging and lifting his hands palm up.

'*Stronger than steel and softer than silk,*' repeated Lana. 'That doesn't make any sense.'

'Neither does the rest of it,' replied Harrison.

'No conferring!' roared the Spider Queen.

Lana took a few small steps away from Harrison, as if to prove they weren't cheating. She glanced at Elvis, who now began a series of elaborate mimes.

'What does that mean?' whispered Lana out of the corner of her mouth.

'It means: Don't. Ask. Me,' replied Elvis breathlessly.

Lana shook her head. Knowing the Spider Queen as she did, it had to be something to do with spiders . . .

Wait! Could *that* be the answer – a spider?

As soon as you fight me the battle is lost. Maybe the answer was the Spider Queen herself? After all, if Lana failed to solve the riddle, everything would be lost. She'd be bundled up in golden thread with Harrison and left in the larder with the other cocoons, while the Spider Queen destroyed Gudrun's village.

But then just as she was beginning to panic, a thought flickered in her brain.

Golden thread!

That had been stronger than steel when it was attached to her finger, and soft as silk when it was woven into a cocoon around her . . .

Could that be the answer? But was it also drier than dust and wetter than milk?

Yes! Back at the marsh, as a spider, the thread she'd pulled from her body had been liquid, and had dried quickly in the air! Drier than dust and wetter than milk!

The answer *must* be the golden thread!

She was about to shout it out triumphantly when a part of her drew back. What about the last two clues? *I hide in the summer and show in the frost, as soon as you fight me the battle is lost.*

Okay, Lana thought, taking a long, slow breath.

Think carefully. It has something to do with spiders, and thread, that you can't see in summer, but you can see in winter? And which, if you fought it, you would lose?

Her mind jumped to the unicorn in the snow, netted by a tangle of golden thread and struggling to break free.

And then . . .

She had the answer!

CHAPTER TWENTY-FIVE

'A web!' declared Lana triumphantly. 'The answer is a web!'

The Spider Queen started in surprise, as a deathly silence descended on the entire room. Narrowing her eyes, she arched over Lana.

'Explain,' she spat.

Lana swallowed hard.

'I think . . .' she began, suddenly uncertain.

She decided to put one word in front of another and see what came out.

'A web can be stronger than steel and softer than silk,' she began. 'Trust me, I've been caught in one.' She cast a glance at Elvis, who shrugged. 'And the thread that makes a web starts out liquid. I know that because I've been a spider.'

She paused, scouring the Spider Queen's face for information. But it was blank.

'I vanish in summer, and loom in the frost,' she continued. 'That's also like a web. When it's warm, you can't see it, which is why flies get stuck. But in winter, you can, because of the frost.'

Once again, Lana searched the Spider Queen's face, but it was as still as a mask.

'And as soon as you fight a web, you've lost, because you just get *more* stuck. So that's it. The answer to your riddle is: a web.'

There was a long pause, then, with the slightest of nods, the Spider Queen admitted defeat. It was the tiniest of gestures, but one that every creature in the Great Chamber noticed, even the Maintenance Spiders, dressed in overalls and hard hats and seated right at the back.

'She's done it!' cried Elvis. 'The queen is deposed. Long live the queen!'

Applause broke out across the Great Chamber, mixing with gasps of surprise and loud mutterings of disbelief.

'Bravo!' called the angry spider, who was now Lana's most enthusiastic supporter. 'Bravo!'

Back on the stage, the Spider Queen closed her eyes and inhaled deeply. She was shrinking! Dark fur was sprouting over her face, and when she opened her eyelids, there were four beady black eyes crammed in each socket. She was turning into a spider herself!

'Congratulations, my dear,' she said with a thin smile. 'I believe this now belongs to you.'

Two spidery arms emerged from beneath her cloak. She carefully removed the gold necklace and offered it to Lana.

'This collar,' she said haughtily, even though she was now no taller than Lana's waist, 'holds all my power. Here.'

But Lana shook her head. 'No,' she said firmly. 'I don't want your powers, or your throne.' Then turning to the audience, she said, 'I just want us to talk. Spiders and humans. Come and meet the villagers' leader, Gudrun. You can trust her, I promise.'

A murmur of agreement rippled across the assembled spiders. Then Harrison's voice rang out.

'The ceiling!' he shouted. 'It's leaking!'

The roof was buckling, and a steady trickle of water was falling, forming a puddle on the stage. Then, as Lana watched, two more leaks burst overhead, sprinkling her with water! Now that the Spider Queen had removed her necklace, her magic was fading fast. Not only had she changed back into a spider, but the thin silk walls of the palace could no longer hold back the lake.

'The villagers!' Harrison remembered. 'We have to get them out before the palace collapses!'

'And the housekeeping spider,' added Lana. 'The one I put a glass over!'

There was a loud creaking sound as the ceiling began to buckle. Jets of water now sprang through the holes, showering down onto humans and spiders alike.

'Elvis!' called Lana, thinking quickly. 'Where are you?'

'Right here, Ma'am!' came the reply.

'Hands up all those in favour of Elvis becoming their leader!' called Lana, and every spider in the room immediately raised a leg.

'Here!' she urged, snatching up the necklace from the floor and placing it in a circle around Elvis. Within seconds, the tiny spider was transforming into a human!

'You're in charge now,' she bellowed. 'Spiders! Meet your new king!'

'You're kidding me?' spluttered Elvis, now an extremely handsome teenager with a tall black quiff.

As the spiders burst into applause, a huge hole appeared in a nearby wall and a torrent of water flowed across the stage and onto the floor of the Great Chamber, lifting clusters of spiders like tiny rafts.

'This way!' bellowed Elvis, pointing towards the entrance hall.

'Harrison!' shouted Lana. 'Follow me!'

As the spiders scrambled for the exit, Lana and Harrison went stumbling down the passageway. Lana snatched up the upturned glass, releasing the grateful housekeeping spider. Then she and Harrison rushed to the larder, where they found Prince Zephir and the other kidnapped villagers emerging groggily from their cocoons.

'Where are we?' demanded Prince Zephir, placing a wary hand on the hilt of his sword.

'The Spider Queen's palace!' gasped Lana. 'This whole place is filling with water. We need to get out of here, now!'

'Well?' asked Zephir, turning to his stunned troops. 'You heard the girl!'

By the time they reached the Great Chamber,

it was empty of spiders, and water was rushing in from all sides. Gripping Lana and Harrison by the hand, Prince Zephir battled against the current, his warriors wading along behind him.

'That way!' called Lana, pointing to the entrance hall. Soon the water was too deep for their feet to touch the bottom and they had to swim to stay afloat, pushing against the current. By the time they reached the entrance hall, the water had almost reached the ceiling.

'What now?' shouted Harrison.

'Dive!' yelled Lana. 'Follow me!'

Filling her lungs with air, Lana ducked under the water, swimming down towards the patch of darkness that she knew marked the entrance to the Golden Palace. Glancing behind her, she saw Harrison, Prince Zephir and the villagers in her wake, bubbles trailing out behind them like streamers. Soon she was leading them out through the mouth of the building and up to where bright sunshine dappled playfully on the water.

Moments later, they were all bobbing on the surface of the lake, laughing and congratulating one another.

'Lana!' called a familiar voice. Gudrun and King Yashar were rowing towards them, escorted by a gaggle of fishing boats.

Reaching out a hand, King Yashar pulled Lana aboard, then Harrison. Gallant Prince Zephir was the last to join them, waiting until all his men were safely out of the water before climbing up himself.

When he did, Gudrun gave him a huge hug, delighted that her long-lost husband had finally been returned to her.

'You're alive!' She beamed, wiping her eyes. 'You're alive!'

'Thanks to these two,' replied Prince Zephir, grinning at Harrison and Lana. 'Hello, brother,' he said, pumping Yashar's hand.

'What happened?' asked Gudrun as King Yashar took the oars and began rowing them back towards the waiting village. 'One minute a marauding bear broke free of the stocks, saving my son . . .' She laughed, and King Yashar smiled broadly. 'The next, he was turning into my brother-in-law!'

'It was Lana,' said Harrison proudly. 'She beat the Spider Queen and took away her magic! Hello – I'm Harrison, by the way.'

As he spoke, the sound of voices drifted across the calm blue water. Shading her eyes from the sun, Lana saw that the bank was lined with villagers, waving and cheering, with Kyle front and centre, leaping up and down.

'I am so sorry,' continued Gudrun, touching

Lana's arm, 'that I didn't believe you. And I'm so grateful that you risked everything to save us all. How can we ever repay you?'

Lana smiled.

'It's not me you need to repay,' she replied. 'It's the spiders.'

CHAPTER TWENTY-SIX

'All clear,' declared Kyle proudly. He was standing knee-deep in the lake, calling to Lana and Harrison on the shore. 'No spiders at all! Just oysters!'

'We know,' replied Lana, rolling her eyes.

'That's the whole point,' said Harrison. They'd only been working for a few minutes, but he and Lana had already had enough of Kyle bossing them around.

'Harrison and Lana,' ordered Kyle, in an important-sounding voice. 'Place your markers.'

Harrison sighed and wedged his stake in the bank. Lana tried to do the same, but instead of grains, the sand was made up of lots of tiny stones, and it was difficult to get the stake to stand up properly.

'That's not deep enough!' called Kyle, marching towards her. 'It's really important that everyone sees these markers! The space between them is the only place humans are allowed to fish. Give it to me, I'll do it.'

For a brief moment, Lana considered reminding Kyle that this whole plan – rebuilding the village destroyed by the storm in a new spot further along the lake, where there were no spiders – had been her idea. But then she thought better of it. They were supposed to be living in harmony, and that included her and Kyle.

'Easy,' said Kyle, confidently, stepping back from the stake, which wobbled then fell over. 'Oh,' he said in a small voice. 'I see what you mean.'

'Can I help?' asked Prince Zephir, striding towards them from the half-finished village.

'We're marking out the fishing area, like you asked me to,' said Kyle importantly.

'Good lad.' Prince Zephir ruffled Kyle's hair and smiled. 'He's not bossing you around too much, is he?' he asked, winking at Harrison and Lana.

'No,' said Harrison quickly. Kyle might be annoying, but he didn't want to get him in trouble.

'Absolutely not,' confirmed Lana.

'Great. Then come and join us in the Great Hall.' Prince Zephir grunted, putting all his weight on the stake. 'Can you and Harrison stay a little longer? Your friend the Spider King is guest of honour.'

'Have we got time?' asked Lana.

'You've at least another hour,' confirmed Prince Zephir. 'By my reckoning, at least.'

Lana paused, thinking it over. The Hollow Tree was their only way home, and at nine o'clock the builders would have a new saw, ready to cut it down. But they couldn't leave without saying a proper goodbye.

'We'd love to,' she said and grinned.

But as they arrived among the crowd of happy villagers milling around the Great Hall, from a nearby section of forest came the sound of voices. Riding on horseback, King Yashar emerged from among the trees, leading the Warden and his three guards, their hands tied.

'Look who I found!' called King Yashar. 'Hiding in my cave!'

'Shame on you, Warden!' called Prince Zephir.

'Leaving your charges to perish in the storm. Put him in the stocks!'

Two broad-shouldered men stepped forward, Lana recognizing them as kidnapped warriors. A look of horror flickered on the Warden's face. 'And be a sitting target for dog sick, chicken poo, and the brown water in the bottom of the lavatory-brush holder? Never!' he cried, leaping from his horse and running off across the sand.

'Irritating man,' muttered King Yashar, whirling three leather-bound weights around his head, then flinging them through the air so that they wrapped neatly round the Warden's ankles, dragging him to the ground.

'No!' begged the Warden. 'Please, please, no!'

'Wait!' called Lana. Approaching the Warden, she looked him straight in the eye. 'Are you sorry for what you've done?'

The Warden shrugged.

'Clearly not,' proclaimed Zephir. 'Seize him!'

'Let him speak!' demanded Lana, stepping between the Warden and the two burly warriors. 'Well?' she pressed, turning to the Warden.

'I guess,' he offered.

Lana cast him a penetrating stare.

'Okay, I admit it,' said the Warden grudgingly. 'It wasn't my finest moment.'

'You see?' declared Lana to Prince Zephir. 'He's sorry. And ashamed. And a little bit disgusted with himself.'

'That's not what I said,' began the Warden, but Lana held up her hand, silencing him, just as Carl Ellis had done to Yashar at their first meeting.

'And in the future, he's going to try and think about people . . . and creatures . . .' She and King Yashar exchanged a meaningful look. 'Other than himself.'

King Yashar shrugged. 'Maybe it's time we all had a fresh start,' he admitted.

'Not too fresh,' countered Prince Zephir. 'After lunch, the four of you can move the village dump.'

Lana would never forget the glorious breakfast they ate that day in the Great Hall. Its huge front doors had been thrown wide open and inside the villagers were hugging and chattering excitedly, delighted to be together again. Sunlight streamed onto a banquet table decorated with green leaves and forest flowers and groaning with every kind of delicious food you could possibly imagine. There were pastries and cakes, hunks of delicious sourdough bread and porridge loaded with nuts and fruits, all washed down with gallons of the most delicious goat's milk.

Elvis was seated at the head of the table, with Gudrun and Lana either side, and the rafters above were festooned with streamers of golden spider-silk, woven by dozens of hard-working spiders, some of whom Lana recognized from her extraordinary adventure. As they ate, everyone discussed their plans for humans and spiders to live in peace. Then finally, as they tucked into their dessert of baked apples stuffed with forest fruits – which was one of Lana's all-time favourites – Gudrun stood up and clanked her cup with her spoon, asking for everyone's attention.

'I can't let this moment pass,' she announced, 'without thanking three people. Firstly, our honoured guest, Elvis, the King.'

'Elvis, Elvis!' chanted the villagers, and he

pushed back his slick of black hair, stood, and bowed his head in acknowledgement.

Gudrun continued, 'When others hurt us, we often seek revenge. Elvis, that was the course your queen pursued, to all of our cost. Thank you for learning with me that only talking can truly solve our problems. With your help, I hope we can put the mistakes of the past behind us and learn to live together. To Elvis!'

Gudrun raised her glass and every villager in the Great Hall did the same.

'Secondly, King Yashar.' All heads turned to the other end of the table, where King Yashar and Kyle sat at either side of Prince Zephir. 'You came here at my request, to help this village in its hour of need, and we returned the favour by scapegoating you, hunting you and imprisoning you in the stocks. Thank you for your wisdom and forgiveness. And thank you, also, for your bravery, in saving our dear son Kyle last night. King Yashar!'

Once again, the room echoed with chants, as every villager raised their drinks, Kyle leaning right across the table to clash his glass against King Yashar's.

'And finally,' said Gudrun, turning to Lana, 'to our mysterious visitor. Your adventure started, I am told, with a single golden thread, fastened to your finger by the Spider Queen. A thread that led you here from another world, to rescue your brother Harrison. That thread has bound us all together. Please accept this small gift, crafted by your beloved Golden Diving Bell spiders, on behalf of us all, as a small token of our gratitude.'

As Gudrun spoke, she gestured for Lana's hand, then slipped a slim gold bracelet onto her wrist. Like the Spider Queen's necklace, it was wound from countless threads of golden spider silk.

'Let this bracelet be a reminder that, from now on, we are stuck in one another's stories. To Lana!'

'The best sister ever!' chirped Harrison, raising his glass.

'Lana, Lana!' repeated the villagers, clapping their hands in unison, and as she looked around the smiling faces that surrounded her, Lana felt her heart flutter with joy.

Soon it was time to leave. They said their goodbyes to the villagers, hugged Elvis, touched elbows with Carl and his three guards (whose hands were not really in a shakeable state after clearing the town dump), and listened patiently to another of Kyle's stories before hugging him too. Then Lana and Harrison set off on horseback with Gudrun, Prince Zephir and King Yashar. They rode up through the forest, past the stream where Lana had first met the bear, up over the ridge and into the Hidden Valley.

The snow had melted, and the clearing that surrounded the Hollow Tree was now a lush meadow, dotted with red poppies and blue cornflowers. There were bees buzzing among the wildflowers and insects dancing in the shade of the trees. High above their heads, a familiar shape wheeled in the wind. The Spider Queen's spell had been lifted.

'Look!' called Lana. 'It's the kite!'

'He's come to say goodbye,' said King Yashar. 'As, I'm afraid, must we.'

'But what if we can't get back?' asked Lana, feeling a pang of anxiety. 'We might never see you again.'

'Just touch your bracelet,' said Gudrun gently, hugging her tightly. 'And we'll be right there with you.'

King Yashar and Prince Zephir lifted them up into the boughs of the tree, and Lana and Harrison hauled themselves upwards, branch by mossy branch. They paused in the crown to wave at their friends below and call out one final goodbye. Then they took one last look at the Hidden Valley, full of life and sunshine, and climbed down into the darkness.

CHAPTER TWENTY-SEVEN

For a few seconds after she woke, Lana had no idea where she was. Everything was so bright, it took her a moment to realize she was lying in a shaft of sunlight, as the early-morning sun poured in through a gap in her bedroom curtains. One by one, familiar objects gradually came into focus. There, hanging on the back of the door, was her unicorn dressing gown. At the end of the bed sat Ted, her gruff-looking teddy bear. On the wall behind him hung one of Nana's Elvis posters. And lying open on the bedside table was her well-thumbed copy of *Beowulf*. She was back in her bed, at Nana and Grandad's house!

As she stretched, she mentally tried to retrace her steps. After saying their goodbyes to Gudrun, King Yashar and Prince Zephir, she and Harrison had climbed back down the inside of the Hollow Tree. But she had no memory of walking back across the marsh and climbing into bed. How had she ended up here?

Confused and still sleepy, she picked up the book. There was the village, just as it had been in her adventure: a collection of wooden huts beside a wide sky-blue lake, nestling in a snow-capped valley of green firs. Had she dreamed the whole thing?

A loud mechanical noise rattled in through her

half-open window, jolting her back to reality. Frowning, she pushed back the curtains and peered out at the marsh. The Hollow Tree was still standing! Studying it closer, she saw that Carl and his three workers were gathered beside its horrified-looking face, wielding a brand-new, motorized saw!

There was no time to waste. She shoved her arms into her dressing gown, charged out onto the landing and burst through Harrison's bedroom door.

'Harrison!' she urged, shaking her brother by the shoulder. 'Wake up!'

Harrison opened one eye. 'Lana,' he said grumpily, examining the hands of his bedside alarm clock. 'It's early – and it's the holidays.'

'I know!' hissed Lana. 'But there's something we have to do.'

'What's that?' he asked wearily, sitting up in bed.

'They're cutting down the Hollow Tree!'

Harrison shrugged. 'I know,' he said matter-of-factly. 'I was there when they told us, remember? You didn't really think that creepy builder guy was going to save it for you?'

'I mean right now – we have to save it! Think of all the insects that live there. And the birds that nest in it. And the spiders that live in the marsh.'

'Since when do you care about spiders?' asked Harrison, bemused.

'Since last night!' insisted Lana. 'Our adventure, remember?'

Harrison shook his head. 'Lana, I'm not going to the Hollow Tree just so you can climb it before they cut it down.'

'What?' asked Lana. 'Don't tell me you've

273

forgotten? I woke up with a golden thread tied to my finger, and when we followed it, you got kidnapped by the Spider Queen, but then a bear helped me and I got you back and we saved all the spiders.'

Harrison sighed. 'Lana, it's way too early to listen to one of your stupid stories.'

'But it's true!'

'Prove it.' Harrison folded his arms, deeply unimpressed. Lana thought desperately – she had to convince her brother to come with her.

She gasped, remembering the bracelet. For a few anxious seconds she searched her wrist, finding nothing, then suddenly there it was. Tucked underneath the sleeve of her pyjama top was a gossamer-thin cord of entwined golden threads, glinting in the sunlight.

'Look!' she said triumphantly, holding it close for Harrison to see. 'What's this?'

'A bracelet?' asked Harrison.

'What's it made of?'

Harrison shrugged. 'Gold, maybe?'

'Look closer.'

'Really thin gold.'

'It's made of spider-silk. Golden spider-silk. Woven by one-hundred-per-cent real Golden Diving Bell spiders and given to me by Gudrun, the head of the village we saved.'

'Or . . .' said Harrison doubtfully. 'It could be out of a Christmas cracker.'

'Fine,' said Lana, taking a deep breath. 'Believe me or don't believe me, I don't care. What matters is that if we don't do something to stop them, those workers are going to ruin the lives of a load of wild creatures. That's something you've always cared about. So have Nana and Grandad. We can't let them get away with it!'

There was a long pause while Harrison looked at his sister with new eyes. Then a broad smile spread slowly across his face. 'Now that's more like it.' He grinned.

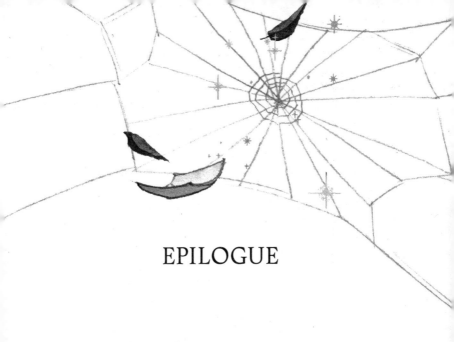

LOCAL FAMILY SAVES SPIDERS!

'Totally irresponsible' was how developer Carl Ellis described the actions of two children and their grandparents last week. 'We've had to delay our building work, at huge cost, all for the sake of some spiders. Frankly, it beggars belief.'

Ellis was complaining about the postponement of the Marsh Lane development, which was delayed after two local children occupied a tree in the centre of the site and refused to come out until the mayor guaranteed that a rare species of spider that lived there could be transported to safety.

Their grandparents, who live close by, supported the protest, providing the children with a steady supply of ginger beer and apple strudel.

The delay the children created was sufficient for local teacher and spider enthusiast Yashar Falarmarzi to obtain an injunction, forbidding building work until the spiders can be moved, based on the expert testimony of spider specialist, Professor North.

When asked why she took direct action, nine-year-old Lana commented, 'Nature is like a web. If you get rid of one creature, all the others will suffer. We need to look after *all* animals, not just the cute and cuddly ones. And that includes spiders.'

A BRIEF NOTE
ABOUT SPIDERS

There's no such thing, sadly, as the Golden Diving Bell spider. But they aren't exactly made up, either . . .

Firstly, Diving Bell spiders do exist. Just like the ones in this story, they live most of their lives underwater, building a dome from silk that they fill with air bubbles collected by their body hair. The main difference is their silk isn't gold; it's silver.

Gold silk is produced, however, by the golden orb weaver spider, which lives in Madagascar. The silk of this extraordinary creature has even been harvested to make clothes: in 2012, a golden cape – just like the Spider Queen's – was exhibited at the Victoria and Albert Museum in London, made from the silk of 1.2 million individual spiders.

Ballooning isn't something I made up, either. Many species fly this way, firing strands of thread into the air that fan out and then carry them away on the wind. One of the first people to report this was Charles Darwin, who saw spiders landing on his ship, *The Beagle*, some sixty miles off the coast of Argentina, on Halloween 1832.

As for girl spiders eating boy spiders, wrapping them in thread, injecting them with digestive juices, then sucking them up like a smoothie ... that's true too! Widow spiders, for example, get their name because the females sometimes eat the males.

Although most spiders have rather poor eyesight, some have better vision than humans. These are the jumping spiders, and they catch their food by creeping up and leaping on top of it. Their vision isn't quite a sharp as ours, but they can see more colours than we can. Most jumping spiders are small – around the size of a housefly – so the fact they can see in such detail is truly impressive.

Lastly, one thing that most definitely isn't made up is the importance of spiders to the ecosystem. Spiders are what we call a keystone species, meaning that they increase the diversity in their habitats by preying on insects that would otherwise eat all the vegetation. And Professor North is right; without them, we would struggle to grow crops.

ACKNOWLEDGEMENTS

Special congratulations go to Lauren Digby, winner of the 2022 Fun Kids Radio competition, for her brilliant and magical story, *The Day Ben Got Stuck In The Fun Kids Studio*. I loved it!

First thanks must go to our neighbours, Chris and Clare Benson, for giving us permission to walk our dogs on their farmland during lockdown. On one of our outings, we discovered a creepy-looking hollow tree with a face that turned out to be a portal to another world...

Thanks also to Sarah and Anselm Guise for introducing me to rewilding and encouraging me to read George Monbiot's fiercely beautiful book *Feral*. Anselm and Sarah live at Elmore Court, one of the country's most sought-after wedding venues, and have returned a sizeable chunk of their land to an uncultivated Valhalla.

Our conversation inspired me to join wildlife photographer Hamza Yassin on an expedition to the Bamff Estate in Perthshire, which was filmed as part of the More4 series *Scotland: Escape to the Wilderness*. Like Elmore Court, the Bamff Estate teems with all sorts of plants, insects, and wild animals that you wouldn't normally find in a cultivated landscape. All these encounters informed the themes in this story, and I would like to thank Hamza for his expertise and friendship, the Ramsay family for their vision, and Allanah Langstaff and her team at Hello Halo for creating such a fascinating programme.

I'm grateful as always to my wife Jessica for her love and support, to my children Jackson, Harrison, and Lana whose exploits continue to inspire the characters in these books, and to my parents Mick and Marion Miller, on who Nana and Grandad are based, right down to the ginger beer and apple strudel. Thanks also to my sister Bronwen Miller Christian and my brother-in-law Phil Christian for their help and advice concerning local government and town planning.

It's a joy to be allowed to run feral in Rachel Denwood's sun-dappled glade at Simon and Schuster Children's, and am deeply grateful to be supported by a thriving ecosystem in the shape of: my brilliant editor Lucy Pearse and her crack editorial team of Katie Lawrence, Anna Bowles, and Leena Lane; my inspirational illustrator Daniela Terrazini; The outstanding S&S Children's design department, with special thanks to Chris Naylor and Sorrel Packham; the peerless Sophie Storr in production; Kat McKenna, Eve Wersocki Morris, Ian Lamb, and Sarah Macmillan in the endlessly creative marketing and publicity department; and Laura Hough, Dani Wilson, Leanne Nulty, Richard Hawton, Nicholas Hayne, Caitlin Withey, and their world-class sales teams.

It is also a privilege to be occasionally captured and tagged by my all-seeing literary agent Luigi Bonomi and his dynamic team at LBA Books; thanks also to Clementine Ahearne and Alice Natali at the indefatigable Intercontinental Literary Agency for introducing me to so many international readers. And while I'm at it, thanks as always to my super-powered acting agents Samira Davies, Alice Burton, and Geri Spicer at Independent Talent Group; to my ever-inventive publicist Clair Dobbs and her superb team at CLD Communications; and to the insurpressably effervescent Rosie Robinson who runs my social media.

Lastly, a heartfelt thank you to my readers. It is a leaping joy to write these stories, and most of that is because of your enthusiasm, imagination, and open heartedness. As the world emerges from its hibernation, I look forward to meeting more of you at bookshops, schools, and book festivals, and answering more of your fantastic questions such as: 'What is the yuckiest thing you have ever eaten?', 'Were you naughty at school?' and 'Why were you so sad in *Paddington*?'

Turn the page for a special sneak peek of Ben's next action-packed magical adventure . . .

Coming
September 2023!

Chapter One

'Did you hear ANY of what I just said?'

Marcus was in the headmaster's office, again, seated between his Mum and Dad, a bored expression on his face.

'Well?' said Mr Strickland, impatiently, glaring at Marcus through his little round glasses. 'I'm waiting.'

'Marcus,' said Mum, putting a hand on Marcus's arm, 'the headmaster is asking whether there might be a reason you keep misbehaving. Something you'd . . . you'd like to tell us? Something you're upset about perhaps?'

Marcus scowled. 'I'm *fine*,' he said.

'You see?' said the headmaster, throwing up his hands in exasperation. 'This is the whole problem, right here. The boy must know he's in serious trouble, but look at him! He just sits there, not a care in the world, like he's waiting for a film to start. Demerits, detentions – it's all just water off a duck's back. I'm sorry, but I think we've reached the end of the road.'

'What are you saying?' asked Mum, sitting bolt upright in her chair.

'I am recommending to the Governors that Marcus is suspended.'

'*Suspended?*' echoed Mum. 'But . . . but . . .'

'Oh come *on*!' said Marcus's dad with a snort. 'Is that really necessary? All he did was move the 'shallow end' sign. It was a joke, wasn't it, Marcus? Just a bit of harmless fun.'

'Not for Mr Figgis, it wasn't. He lost two front teeth demonstrating a racing dive.'

Dad stifled a laugh, and Mum shot him a stern look.

'I'm sorry,' frowned the headmaster, straightening his glasses. 'Do you find that amusing?'

'Nope,' replied Dad innocently, struggling to keep a straight face. 'Nothing funny about that!' He gave his son a little nudge in the ribs and shot him a knowing wink.

'I would remind you,' continued Mr Strickland, reaching for Marcus's file, 'that this is not Marcus's first incident. This term alone, your son has been caught . . .' He opened the front cover, licked his finger, and located the appropriate page. 'Putting laxatives in the school custard, shaving the school goat, spray-painting obscene images on the staffroom door, and let me see, oh yes, substituting potassium for sodium in one of Mrs

Brightwell's chemistry demonstrations thereby causing a SERIOUS explosion.'

As if closing the subject, Mr Strickland shut the file and glared through his thick-framed glasses across the desk once more.

'Trust me,' said Dad, chuckling, 'when I was at school, I did a lot worse.'

'This is no laughing matter,' snipped Mr Strickland. 'Mrs Brightwell's eyebrows may never grow back.'

'Graham, please,' said Mum, leaning across the desk and looking pleadingly into the headmaster's eyes. 'Something like this . . . It could really affect Marcus's future. Just give him one more chance.'

But Mr Strickland was unmoved. 'I'm sorry, Mrs Watts,' he replied curtly. 'I've made my decision.'

'Fourteen years I've taught here . . .'

'I don't see that that's releva—'

'Fourteen years!' Mum said again, louder this time. 'The last three of which, I've been acting

Head of History, with twice the work and no extra pay. As well as running the Bring and Buy sale at the school fair *and* the Year 6 orienteering course. Marcus isn't a bad kid, you *know* that. He's just going through a rough time. You're sorry, aren't you, Marcus? And you promise you won't do it again, don't you?'

Mum reached desperately across the table and grabbed Mr Strickland's hand. 'I know he needs punishing, Graham – but he needs help too. Maybe there's somewhere we can send him over half term? Some sort of tutor, or therapist, or camp, or—'

Mr Strickland looked up suddenly, as if an idea had occurred to him.

Mum paused, watching him carefully.

'Hmm,' said Mr Strickland.

'Hmm?' repeated Mum, hopefully.

Removing the handkerchief from his top suit pocket, Mr Strickland gave both lenses of his glasses a long and thoughtful clean. Then repositioning them back on his nose, he said, 'Well, there is *one* place.'

'Oh thank you, Graham!' said Mum, pushing back her chair and rushing round the other side of the desk to give the headmaster a hug. 'We'll try anything . . . thank you. You won't regret this, I promise.'

Mr Strickland blushed and shooed her away. 'Now, now, I'm not making any promises. We'll have to call and see if they have room. It's a rather . . . unconventional place. Their methods are . . . unusual, to say the least.'

'What's it called?' asked Mum.

But Mr Strickland didn't answer. Instead, he reached for the corner of his desk, lifted an old-fashioned telephone from its cradle, and dialled.

'Mrs Pettifer, I'd like to place a call please. To the admissions team . . .' he glanced at Marcus's Mum. 'At Merlin's.'